But was Sa
nothing in ret

In every way, he had behaved as a gentleman should. But why? What did he have to gain? What did he want from them, *from her*, in exchange?

She couldn't deny that every time she was near him her breath came a little faster and her heart began to trip and stall. The way he had with the children, even the prickly Phin, made her middle feel mushy and warm, and sometimes when he looked right at her she forgot to breathe altogether.

Stop it, Eldora. You're in danger of making a complete fool of yourself. A man like Sam Mackenzie would never be interested in an ugly duckling like you, poorer than a muskrat, with no proper schooling. If you let yourself dream romantic notions about him, you're just going to get your heart broken when he leaves you in Denver. Get through the next two days with your wits and your heart intact.

Something tugged her sleeve. She looked down into Tick's face.

"I said, 'He's pretty swell, isn't he?'"

She smoothed his fair hair out of his eyes and nodded, a lump in her throat. "Yes, he's pretty swell, but Tick..."

Light to My Path

Erica Vetsch

Heartsong Presents

To Mr. David Heter, teacher and friend, who nutured my love of words and books and who encouraged me to write. Thank you for your guidance and all the prayers you prayed for me.

A note from the Author:
I love to hear from my readers! You may correspond with me by writing:

Erica Vetsch
Author Relations
PO Box 721
Uhrichsville, OH 44683

ISBN 978-1-61626-447-5

LIGHT TO MY PATH

All scripture quotations are taken from the King James Version of the Bible.

This book is a work of fiction. Names, characters, places, and incidents are either products of the author's imagination or used fictitiously.

Our mission is to publish and distribute inspirational products offering exceptional value and biblical encouragement to the masses.

PRINTED IN THE U.S.A.

one

He should've known she was hiding something. From the moment Sam Mackenzie had asked Yvette Adelman to marry him, something had been wrong. Only he'd been too besotted by her beauty to want to dig any deeper, which compounded his foolishness.

Sam tilted his head toward the conversation in the next room and considered the old adage about eavesdroppers never hearing any good about themselves. If that wasn't the plain truth. He blew out a breath and wondered at which point he should push the door open and confront his fiancée and her mother. Maybe he'd best listen a little more and make sure he had heard right.

"I won't have any trouble. Sam Mackenzie is an absolute sheep and too dumb to realize it." Yvette's lyrical tones belied the insulting words.

Sam's mouth twisted, and his chest felt hollow.

"He's loaded. That's all that matters." Hortense Adelman's voice carried across the drawing room and through the inch-wide gap in the pocket doors. For a tiny woman, she sure had a powerful speaking voice. He hadn't been at all sorry at the thought of leaving his soon-to-be mother-in-law behind in a few days.

"He adores me." Yvette laughed. "I've only to mention that I want something, and he's around here with it in a trice. And he's eager. I barely had to suggest moving the

5

wedding date up, and he pounced on the idea. In two days I'll be Mrs. Sam Mackenzie, we'll be on a train for Colorado, and I'll be rich. A few weeks in the Mackenzie mansion in Martin City—doesn't that sound like a dreadful frontier hamlet?—then I'll tell him how homesick I am for St. Louis, how much I need my mother. I'll be back here by Easter. Once I'm in the city, I can put off returning to Colorado indefinitely. I'll have money to burn. By next fall, things will be settled, and I'm sure I can be back in St. Louis society with no one the wiser."

"What about Anthony? You won't see him anymore, will you? That would ruin everything. If Sam caught you two together, everything would explode."

"Oh pooh, I could explain Anthony to Sam. Sam would believe whatever I told him."

Sam's neck muscles knotted, and his throat tightened. The bouquet he held shook, and his thumb made a crease in the foil cover of the chocolate box. He eased them onto the table beside the door.

"I'm still amazed at him appearing in our hour of need, Yvette."

"I told you things would work out fine. I just needed to find the right man to come along. And soon."

Her laugh, one of the things that had first drawn Sam's attention, lilted like music. How could something that looked and sounded so good be such a sham? He squared his shoulders and pushed open the pocket doors. "Good afternoon, Yvette, Hortense."

The way they both jumped would've been comical if he hadn't known what they were up to. Yvette got to her feet, graceful and fluid as always. Sunshine from the bank of windows shone and raced along the fiery ringlets on her cheeks. Her skin, usually white and cool as marble, now showed a hint of color. She widened her sapphire eyes and flicked her lashes. "Why, Sam, I didn't expect you so early." She crossed the room and held out her hands, raising her face for his customary kiss. When he failed to oblige, she pulled back and ducked her chin. "What's this? You're not getting shy practically on the eve of our wedding?" She batted his arm.

"Shy?" He shook his head. "A sheep like me?" Turning from her, he took the chair beside the fireplace. "That is what you called me, isn't it?"

Yvette shot a glance at her mother and then shrugged. "You've been eavesdropping. Darling, you misunderstood. Whatever you thought you heard has been misconstrued." She pursed her lips into a bow and blinked at him, the picture of innocence. From her auburn curls to her kid slippers, everything about her was perfect. The white, frothy dress with blue flowers just the color of her eyes, the cameo threaded on a ribbon around her slender neck, her long, delicate fingers ending in perfectly rounded nails—everything calculated to please a man's eye. She put her hands behind her back in an appealing gesture, one he'd fallen for too many times.

"I don't believe I misunderstood. I believe I understand for the first time." He shook his head. "You've been deceiving me from the minute I met you."

She spread her hands, palms up. "Sam, I can explain."

He looked at Hortense, who sat frozen in her chair, her skin mottled and her mouth slack. "I don't need to hear any more of your lies. This farce of an engagement is over. You'll have to find yourself some other idiot."

Yvette's mouth opened, and a little squeak came out. She shook her lovely head. "No, Sam, you don't mean that. You love me."

A rueful chuckle escaped him. "I sure thought I did. I feel almost as much of a fool as you made me out to be. Suckered by your looks and your pretty talk. I think I was in love with the idea of you, flattered that someone so beautiful would fall for the likes of me. I let you manipulate me, talk me into a short engagement." He shook his head. "I should've known. Something's been off about our relationship from the start. You had me measured up for a matrimonial noose the minute we were introduced."

Hortense gave a strangled cry. "Don't do this to my girl. You'll ruin everything."

"Mother, please leave us alone. I know we can sort this out if we can just be alone for a little while."

Hortense scuttled out of the room as if her hem were on fire. She threw one last desperate glance over her shoulder before closing the doors behind her.

Two perfect tears squeezed out of Yvette's eyes. "Sam, please, I beg you not to do this. Let me explain." She stepped toward him, but he rose and rounded the chair, putting it between him and his ex-fiancée.

"No, it wouldn't be the truth. I think being truthful is beyond your capabilities. You've traded on your looks and gotten favors from men for so long, it's become a habit. You say whatever you think they want to hear. You lie when it suits you, and you deny the truth when confronted." He sighed, giving free rein to all the doubts that had been building over the past month. "This isn't the first time I've caught you lying, but I believed your explanations because I wanted to believe."

Yvette's face crumpled. "Please Sam, say you don't mean the engagement is off. I'll apologize if something I said hurt your feelings. I don't really think you're a sheep. I love you, and I know you love me." She edged around the chair and stroked his arm.

His guts roiled. Where once he had eagerly anticipated her touch, now it felt akin to a snake slithering across his skin. He jerked back. "No. It's over. They say there's a sucker born every minute. Well, I'm all done being your sucker. I used to believe in love. I think that's why I fell for you so quickly in the first place. I *wanted* to fall in love. But being with you has cured me of that notion for good."

Yvette dissolved into sobs, though he noted how controlled and perfect her crying appeared and how every few seconds she glanced reproachfully at him, as if she were gauging his response for signs of capitulation. More games, more lies.

Sam brushed past her and shoved the doors open.

Hortense jumped aside and pressed against the wall opposite the doors, her hand on her chest.

He grabbed his hat and the flowers and chocolates. Jamming his hat on his head, he couldn't resist one last jab. "Baa!"

જ

Eldora Carter kept her chin up and refused to cry, though the tears burning the backs of her eyes demanded release. Staring straight ahead, hands clasped in front of her, she tried to be brave in the face of the tirade coming from her employer.

"I will not stand for this impertinence." Mrs. Gamble's bulk nearly overwhelmed the chair. She placed her pen into its holder and leaned back. "You will apologize to my son, and you will remember your place in this household." She crossed her arms under her broad bosom and contemplated the pelmet. "This is what I get for my charity. I told Mr. Korbin I wanted someone who would know her place, do her work, and not cause me any trouble. And he sends me you." Her hand waved in a dismissive gesture. "Dressed like a scarecrow, eyes like saucers, and no sense of what being a domestic requires."

Eldora adjusted her shawl, crossing it over her chest like armor. Her hands stung from the hours of scrubbing she'd already put in today, and her lower back ached from her time over the washtubs.

"You've been here three weeks, and this is the third time I've had to reprimand you." Mrs. Gamble's eyes looked small in her puffy face. Like a colt, she had fine whiskers around her lips that quivered when she was angry. They quivered now. "I don't know what they taught you at that orphanage, and I suppose I should've expected no better, but for you to try to entice my son is beyond the scope of common decency."

Beau Gamble hadn't even had the courage to own up to what he had done. Was the red mark of her hand still evident on his cheek? She hoped so. The lout. She swallowed against the lump in her throat and returned her attention to Mrs. Gamble.

"I will not tolerate such behavior under my roof. If you want to comport yourself as a common trollop, you will do so elsewhere. You will apologize to my son and give me your promise you will behave yourself, or I'll send you straight back to the orphanage, and Conrad can deal with you."

Eldora said nothing. She shifted her weight, trying to ease the discomfort on the bottom of her right foot where the sole of her boot had worn through. She'd stepped on a sharp stone on her way to the grocery for the cook this morning, and the resulting bruise throbbed.

"Well, are you going to apologize?"

She finally looked her employer in the eye. Though her mouth was dry, she refused to back down. "No ma'am, I am not. I have nothing to apologize for."

Mrs. Gamble blinked and gasped. Her mouth slacked, and for a moment the whiskers stopped trembling. "What do you call throwing yourself at my son like a tart?"

"I did no such thing. Your son is the one to blame." Even as she said it, Eldora knew it was useless to protest her innocence. Mrs. Gamble would never believe her precious son could be lascivious. Any trouble would always be the fault of the girl. But she refused to be accused any longer without standing up for herself.

"Your son is the most disgusting man I've ever met. I couldn't walk from my room to the basement laundry without him accosting me. His suggestions and comments were filthy. Why do you think you have such trouble keeping help in this house? It's your awful son. He tried several times to kiss me, but I managed to evade him. Today, I'd finally had enough. He deserves worse than a slap across his horrible face, and if you don't put a stop to his actions he'll go on until he finally ruins some poor girl. Well, I refuse to be that girl."

Mrs. Gamble's eyes glittered like a snake's. "You lie. All you servant girls are alike. You try to capture a man, and when he rebuffs you, you make wild accusations." She levered herself up and stood toe-to-toe with Eldora.

Though Eldora's insides quaked, she refused to show fear. She might be about to be turned out into the cold, but she would not cower before this tyrant. "It is you who is lying to yourself, Mrs. Gamble. I may only be an orphan, and not very pretty. And I have nothing of my own but my dignity and my virtue. But I will give neither to you or your son. I quit."

Mrs. Gamble looked like she might strangle on all she wanted to say.

Before the woman unscrambled her thoughts, Eldora walked out of the sumptuous room. She marched up three flights to her attic bedroom, stuffed her nightgown and comb into her small bag, and headed downstairs. Since she didn't own a coat, her shawl would have to suffice on the long walk.

Beau waited on the landing, his handsome face sneering. She stopped, instantly wary, though taking small satisfaction that the outline of her fingers still showed on his cheekbone. "Leaving? Too bad. I would've liked the chance to tame that feisty temper."

"Let me pass."

"Not without a kiss good-bye."

"You're a rogue and a rake, Beau Gamble. If you touch me I'll scream this house right down."

"Can I carry your bag for you, miss?" The houseman stood at the foot of the steps. His face seemed carved from granite. Relief washed through Eldora even as disappointment flashed in Beau's eyes.

"Yes, please." She edged by Beau and hurried to the first floor.

Jimson took her bag and her elbow. "I'm sorry you're leaving us, miss." The older man tugged her arm when she would've turned to go to the back door. "You'll go out the front, like a lady." He kept looking straight ahead, but his expression softened somewhat from its usual sternness. Bowing slightly, he held the door for her and handed her the parcel she'd given him. "Godspeed, miss."

"Thank you, Jimson." She smiled and squeezed his arm. It was the first time in her three weeks in the Gamble house that she'd called the man by his name. When he closed the door, she headed down the gravel horseshoe drive toward the street to begin the long walk back to the orphanage.

She stopped when she got to the street and looked back at the mansion. How could something so beautiful on the outside be so rotten on the inside?

two

Eldora trudged up the snow-covered steps to the orphanage, weary, wet, and wishing she could be anywhere else. Entering the front hall, she stomped her numb feet to rid them of their icy encasement. The familiar smells of cooked cabbage, lye soap, and damp wool wrapped around her.

Behind the classroom door on her left muffled recitations emitted, and from the back hall pots clanked and water poured. She turned to her right, determined to get the lecture over with. Her chest tightened. What if he wouldn't take her back? She was of age and had no real right to be at the orphanage any longer. If Mr. Korbin refused her refuge. . .

Please God, let him take me back. I don't have anywhere else to go.

Placing her bundle on the bench beside the door—a bench where children in need of discipline often sat awaiting Mr. Korbin's ire—she tapped. Her knees trembled as the door swung open.

Mrs. Scrabeck wore a smile until she recognized Eldora. Her nostrils flared, and her lips pinched like she'd just kissed a dill pickle. "Eldora Carter, what are you doing here?" She poked her head around the doorjamb and spied the bundle of Eldora's belongings. Her sigh nearly parted Eldora's hair. "Again? Mr. Korbin is not going to like this." She glared, appraising Eldora from her not-quite-blond-not-quite-brown hair to her wet hem and water-spotted shoes. "I suppose you'd better come in, but keep in mind, Mr. Korbin has a board meeting in a few minutes."

Eldora swallowed hard and resisted ducking her head to scuttle in like a mouse. Her cheeks burned, and she pressed her lips together.

Mrs. Scrabeck pointed to a chair before slipping into Mr. Korbin's office. A frosted pane bore his name in black-and-gold letters, and through its semiopaque glass, dark shapes moved.

Eldora clasped her hands in her lap and shut her eyes. Mr. Korbin's voice, deeper and louder than Mrs. Scrabeck's, rose high. Footsteps, and the door crashed open.

"Miss Carter, why are you here? Have you been dismissed again?" He loomed over her, solid and stern, the ultimate authority in her life for the past nine years. "I told you not to return. You had a perfectly good placement with the Gambles."

She cringed and then forced herself to straighten. "Mr. Korbin, I couldn't stay there."

His sigh was even bigger than Mrs. Scrabeck's. "I suppose you had better come into the office." He held the door, and her shoes squished as she dragged into the room. Mr. Korbin took his time rounding the desk and easing down into the plush chair.

Eldora stared at the blotter, heartily sick of being called to account for her shortcomings.

"Go ahead. What was it this time? Impertinence?"

She lifted her chin. "Mrs. Gamble said I was impertinent, but I had to be." The memory of Beau Gamble's hard hands on her, his squishy lips on her neck and cheek, and his pushing her up against the wall made her skin crawl.

"What did you do?"

She loathed the patient forbearance in his voice that said she was nothing more than a nuisance he'd like to scrape off the bottom of his shoe. Heat bloomed in her chest.

"What did *I* do? I refused to let Mrs. Gamble's grown son take advantage of me. He tried to compromise my virtue, and I slapped his face for it. I knew it would cost me my position, and I knew there was every chance you wouldn't take me back here, but I couldn't stand that arrogant man. He deserved worse than a smack. I wish now I'd hit him harder." She trembled, remembering his leers and disgusting suggestions.

Mr. Korbin pressed his lips in a hard line, and his neck went rigid. "You slapped Beau Gamble?" A cough stuck in his throat, and he leaned forward to take a sip from the glass of water on his desk. "Do you realize that Olivia Gamble is one of the most generous patrons this orphanage has? Do you know how many of our orphans she has taken into her home and given jobs?"

"How many of those were girls? How many of them do you think Beau Gamble has ruined? I'm not the first girl he tried his tricks on." Libby and April, the upstairs maids, were afraid of Beau and whispered of another girl who had gotten in the family way as a result of his attentions and was dismissed for low morals. "I would think you'd be more concerned about the welfare of the girls you place out."

Mr. Korbin leaned forward, his eyes like ice. "That's enough. I won't have you spreading vile gossip about the son of one of our patrons. This is the third time you've lost a perfectly good job that would get you out of my hair once and for all, and this is the third time you've come crawling back here. Might I remind you that you are no longer of an age to live at this orphanage? We've done the best we can for you, and it is time you made your own way in this world."

A feeling like sand trickling through fingers started in her chest. How would she make her own way? She had no skills beyond being a domestic, and she had no references without the orphanage's backing. "Are there any other positions available? I assure you, Mr. Korbin, I don't try to get fired. The first one wasn't my fault. The family moved out of the state and didn't wish to take the servants with them. The second time, well, I couldn't stand by and let the housekeeper beat that poor boot boy to death. His transgression didn't warrant getting caned senseless. As for Beau Gamble, you can't tell me you think I should've accepted his advances just to keep the position of laundress?" She shook her head hard enough that a hank of hair came out of its pin and slid over her right eye. With a shove, she tucked it behind her ear. "Not even if I had to sleep on the street in the teeth of a blizzard."

Hands flat on the desktop, Mr. Korbin levered himself up and leaned over the blotter. "Don't take that tone with me, missy. Sleeping on the street isn't outside the realm of possibility for you tonight." He shook his finger, his face a dull red. "You're too old to live here anymore. We've done the best we can for you, placed you with three good employers, and you've managed to lose every position. As of this minute—"

Mrs. Scrabeck knocked on the door and stuck her head inside. "Mr. Korbin, there's a policeman here to see you, and you have a board meeting upstairs in three minutes."

At the mention of a policeman, Eldora's insides sloshed. Surely slapping a lout wasn't a criminal matter. Had Mrs. Gamble set the police after her? She tried to moisten her dry lips, but her mouth was parched.

"Show him in."

When Eldora edged to the door, Mr. Korbin held up his hand. "Wait. I'm not through with you."

A burly police officer entered, pushing the door aside and dragging someone after himself. "Korbin, I thought you were going to keep this one under close watch." He heaved, and Phin Bartholomew skidded into view. His black forelock hung in his eyes, and those eyes glowed like coals through the strands. A dirty smear decorated his swarthy, thin cheek.

Mr. Korbin braced himself on the desk, dropping his head momentarily as if his burdens were too great for one man to bear. "What did he do this time?"

"Caught him down at the grocer's helping himself to the food and folks' wallets."

Phin glared, unrepentant. He kept trying to worm out of the policeman's grasp, but the beefy officer appeared not to notice the attempts, nor did he loosen his ham-fisted grip on Phin's collar.

Eldora's heart went out to the boy. They were both caught in untenable situations with no hope of escaping their fates.

Mr. Korbin walked to the door and summoned Mrs. Scrabeck. "Please take Phin to the matron. She's to see to it he doesn't leave the premises again, and she has free rein to discipline him as she sees fit."

"That old cow can't keep me here, and you can't either." Phin swung out, trying to land a blow with his skinny arms, but the policeman dangled him until he stood on tiptoe. "She can beat me with that radiator brush all she likes, but I'll get away. See if I don't. . . ." Phin protested all the way out of the room.

Eldora closed her eyes, fisting her hands, impotent to change anything for the boy or for herself. The matron, a sour woman who had no fondness for children, would no doubt do as Phin predicted. The radiator brush was a favorite method of discipline in the orphanage.

Mrs. Scrabeck showed the policeman and Phin out and then poked her sour face around the edge of the door. "Sir, your meeting?"

Mr. Korbin turned back to Eldora. "Wait on the bench in the hall until my meeting is over. Then I'll see what's to be done with you."

❧

Sam wanted to shake the dust off his feet when he stepped out of the Adelman house. How could he have been so blind? A sheep, was he? He chuckled. Baa-ing at Hortense had been childish, but it sure had felt good.

He checked his timepiece and waited for a wagon loaded down with barrels to roll by before crossing the street. Plenty of time until he had to meet Great-aunt Tabitha at the orphanage.

Thoughts of his father's aunt brought a smile to his face. No-nonsense, wise, and funny, he had no doubt she would have plenty to say about his broken engagement.

Barges and riverboats lined the shores of the muddy Mississippi, and Illinois lay wreathed in low clouds on the far side of the water. He strolled down Lucas Place toward Missouri Park. As he passed the art museum, he considered stopping in to kill some time, but as stirred up as he was after his confrontation with Yvette, he had no desire to stare at paintings and sculptures. Better to walk off his mood.

Turning up his collar against the brisk wind, he tucked the candy box and flowers under his arm and ambled through the park. Black branches outlined in snow stood starkly against the sky. With less than two weeks until Christmas, bells rang out merrily on passing sleighs, and wreaths hung on many of the front doors of the townhouses that bordered the park.

When he'd gone as far toward the river as he could go without wading, he turned south toward downtown and the orphanage. In just a few days, he'd be back in Colorado, out of this bustling city where he'd spent the last three months and breathing the cold, crisp air of the Rockies. Thoughts of home carried him to the doorstep of the orphanage about ten minutes before Aunt Tabitha's meeting was scheduled to break up.

He entered, noting that the cold had browned the edges of some of the flowers he carried. Fitting, he supposed. He was certainly browned off with Yvette. The hothouse Christmas roses had cost him plenty. How much money had he squandered keeping the acquisitive Yvette happy?

He twisted his mouth and, once inside, glanced around to get his bearings. Humiliation pricked his skin. How was he going to tell his family, who would be expecting him to arrive in a few days as a newlywed, that he'd been suckered by a gold digger with a pretty face?

A girl sat on a bench in the front hall with her feet primly together and her arms anchoring a dun-colored shawl around her thin shoulders. The shawl matched her hair, some of which had slipped from the pleat at the back of her head and lay on her cheek. One of the orphans, no doubt. Maybe fourteen? He scrubbed his feet on the mat, and at the noise, she looked up.

The biggest, light-brown eyes he'd ever seen. He sucked in a breath and nodded to her, touching his hat brim. She was older than he'd thought, though not by a lot. Eighteen or nineteen maybe? Her lashes were gathered into damp points, and when she looked at her lap again, she dabbed at them with the corner of her shawl. More than a few inches of her hem bore water stains and damp spots

He cleared his throat and knocked on the door marked OFFICE. Somewhere upstairs a thumping, pounding ruckus started up with muffled yells. He frowned. Sounded like a stampede.

The girl darted a look up the stairs and twisted her hands

in her lap. Her bottom lip disappeared behind her teeth.

A door opened above, and several whacks rocketed down the steps. "Stop that yelling. You've no one to blame but yourself. If you want more of this brush, then you just keep up your caterwauling. I'll give you something to yell about." The door slammed, making the young woman on the bench flinch.

Sam was of a mind to go upstairs and investigate when the office door opened, and a pinch-nosed woman stuck her face out. "Yes, can I help you?"

"Sam Mackenzie. I'm meeting my aunt here in a few minutes. Miss Tabitha Mackenzie? She's in a board meeting, I believe?"

Her sour expression softened into more pleasant lines. "Of course. Please, come in. Can I get you some coffee?"

Another loud thump upstairs made the gaslight rattle. "What's going on up there? A wrestling match?"

The woman made damping motions with her hands. "I'm sorry. One of the boys is in a bit of trouble, and matron has had her hands full with him for the past hour. Don't worry. She has a way with boys. They need a firm hand, you know."

It sounded as if the matron would make a good prison guard. Whoever the kid was, he felt sorry for the boy.

Sam placed the candy and flowers on the table, wishing he'd disposed of them on the walk over. Still, the inmates at this charming establishment might like a few caramel drops to brighten their existence. Aunt Tabitha could have the flowers. He consulted his watch, comparing it to the clock on the wall.

The secretary went back to her desk, but she darted looks at Sam, making him shift in his seat and rotate his hat in his hands.

When he thought he couldn't stand her furtive glances

any longer, the hall door opened and Aunt Tabitha entered, followed by a tall, spare man with iron-gray hair and black bushy eyebrows that dominated his hatchet face.

The man closed the door to the hall. "It's the perfect solution, and the rest of the directors agree with me. We'll be solving several problems at once."

"I prefer to think of them as children, not problems, Conrad." Aunt Tabitha leaned on her cane. Her voice, though soft, carried a note of steel. " 'Out of sight, out of mind' isn't a solution; it's dereliction of duty." Sam rose, and Tabitha nodded to him but continued to address the hawk-faced man. "I realize I'm new around here and I'm not familiar with all the procedures, but I do know those children deserve better than being shunted off in the middle of the night."

The man—Sam assumed he must be Conrad Korbin as the name on the interior office proclaimed—clenched his jaw as if holding on to the last thread of his patience. "The matter has been decided. You might be grateful the little girl isn't being sent to an asylum. That would be far more in keeping with her condition. They will depart on tomorrow night's train. I'll pen a letter to be delivered upon their arrival in Denver."

Tabitha turned to him. "Sam, I'm sorry to have kept you waiting. What should've been a routine business meeting turned into something else altogether." She lowered her brows at Mr. Korbin. "I've sent for my carriage."

"Hello, Aunt Tabitha." He kissed her offered cheek, breathing in the scent of licorice and lavender, a combination he always associated with her. The tissue paper around the flowers rustled when he picked them up. "These are for you."

She took the roses and buried her nose in the dark-red buds for a moment before tilting her head back to peer at him through her pince-nez. "Not that these aren't delightful, but I have a feeling there's something you need to tell me."

"There is, but we can talk about it on the way to your house." The chocolates remained on the table, and he considered telling the secretary to pass them out to the children, but something about the woman didn't sit well with him. Her pinched mouth and the way she looked down her nose made him think she might be as mean as second-skimmings. He scooped up the candy box and took Tabitha's arm. Escorting her to the hall, he nodded to Korbin and opened the door.

The girl still sat on the bench. Her shoulders sloped as if the entire world bore down on them and a slight hiccup hitched her frame. Poor kid. The atmosphere in this place was more like that of a prison than a home for children. Enough to make anyone cry.

He stopped Tabitha when she moved toward the front door. "Just a minute." Squatting beside the girl, he placed the box of chocolates on her lap.

She looked up, surprising him again with her enormous gingerbread-colored eyes. In a flash, her lashes darted downward as she ducked her chin. Her long, thin fingers traced the Currier and Ives snowscape on the top of the gilt cardboard, and her pink lips parted with a short, sharp intake of breath.

"This is for you. Share it with some of your friends here." He almost chucked her under the chin, but something stayed his hand.

She held herself rigid, as if expecting him to grab her.

Shrugging, he stood and turned to his aunt. As he held the door for her, he glanced over his shoulder.

The girl watched him, her eyes filled with gratitude out of proportion for such a small gift. Her lips moved slightly, enough for him to make out what she said. "Thank you."

He nodded, wishing he could do more for her than a box of candy, and chided himself. He didn't know her situation or anything about her. He had enough women troubles without inviting more.

three

"I'm not asking you to adopt these children. Just ease their way a bit on their journey. They won't be any trouble." Tabitha adjusted the sable stole around her throat and glanced up the depot platform toward the engine. "It's providential, I tell you. You've made a good escape from the clutches of Yvette, and you're traveling on the same train as Miss Carter and the children. You can look in on them from time to time and make sure they all arrive safely in Denver."

Providential didn't exactly fit Sam's description of the situation. "You're taking my broken engagement awfully well." He guided Tabitha to a less-busy corner. "Though I have to admit, the celebratory dinner last night was nice."

Tabitha chuckled. "I never liked Yvette, but you were so taken with her I didn't like to say so. The entire relationship felt so hurried. You barely knew the girl before you got engaged, and the rushed wedding plans didn't sit well. Having Hortense Adelman for a mother-in-law wouldn't have been pleasant either. Hortense is not well received in St. Louis society, and she was using the engagement to get invitations into the best parlors and salons of the city. She'll no doubt have her petticoats in an uproar over the broken engagement."

"Yvette didn't want to wait to be married, and fool that I am, I was flattered by her. . .zeal?" He rubbed his chin and grimaced.

A baggage handler approached them and touched the peak on his cap. "I've placed your bags in your private car at the rear of the train, sir. Is there anything else I can do for you before departure?"

Sam opened his wallet and pulled out a bill. "No, that will be all. Thank you."

The porter eyed the paper and blinked. "Thank *you*, sir." He hastily tucked the money out of sight and backed away with a bow.

"Where is that girl? If they don't get here soon, they'll miss the train." Tabitha leaned on her cane and looked up and down the platform.

The locomotive hissed and clanked, smelling of grease and coal smoke and spewing clouds of steam that hung in the frosty air. Gaslights illuminated the platform, and the milling passengers cast shadows. A baggage cart squeaked by laden with trunks.

"I have grave reservations about what Mr. Korbin is doing with these children, but it's out of my hands. I was outvoted. There are things going on at that orphanage that need looking into. That's why I got myself appointed as a board member last month—though it took a hefty donation to get the matter accomplished. If yesterday's meeting is any indication of how things are run, I shall have to take things in hand and make some changes."

Sam had no doubt she would be running the place inside of three months. Old Korbin wouldn't know what hit him.

"You will keep an eye on the children, won't you?" The lines in her face deepened.

"I'll do my best." He caught the flash of lamplight off russet hair, and his heart jolted. At the same instant, someone bumped his shoulder. He did a nifty two-step to avoid tottering into Aunt Tabitha, all the while keeping his head on a swivel for another glimpse of who he thought he'd seen.

It was her.

And she'd spotted him.

Men stopped to stare after Yvette, but for the first time in his recollection she gave no heed to the admiring glances. Her blue eyes burned like holes in her white face.

Uncertainty swamped him. Was she really taking the breakup so hard? He hadn't thought her emotionally involved at all, or he might not have been so abrupt—not that he regretted his decision. Breaking the engagement had been the right thing to do.

Aunt Tabitha harrumphed and hobbled a few steps away but not before elbowing him and giving him a don't-make-a-fool-of-yourself-again glare. Not that he was of a mind to stick his head back into the bear trap of romance ever again.

"Sam, thank goodness you haven't left yet." Tears hovered on Yvette's coppery lashes. "I need to speak with you."

"I can't see what we have to talk about."

"Please, won't you let me apologize?" A man jostled her on his way by and muttered an apology.

Sparse snowflakes hovered in the air, and Sam realized she wore no hat. "You look cold. Let's go into the waiting room."

He turned to Aunt Tabitha, but she looked past him. "I see Mr. Korbin with the children." She leveled a hard stare at Yvette. "You deal with Miss Adelman, and then come and find me before departure."

Sam took Yvette's elbow and led her into the building. The smell of damp wool and wood smoke curled around him. He spotted a place beside a mountain of luggage where traffic seemed to eddy and flow by. When they reached it, he dropped her arm and crossed his.

She laced her fingers and held them to her chest, her eyes turned upward to him. "Please Sam, won't you reconsider? I'm so sorry for what you heard. I let myself get carried away talking to mother. I don't really think you're a sheep. I don't know why I said that." She reached out to touch his forearm and flicked her lashes. "Don't you remember all we meant to each other? You feel something for me. I know you do. Please, tell me you'll still marry me." She leaned close, eyes full of appeal.

Another pair of eyes interposed itself in his memory. Big, brown eyes, as honest as the day was long. Brown eyes so grateful for a simple box of chocolates that he'd felt warmed through. Yvette's appeal only left him cold and ashamed that he'd ever been duped by her facade.

He leaned back. "It's over, Yvette. I accept your apology, for what it's worth, but I have no intention of marrying you. You'll have to look elsewhere for your sacrificial lamb."

"I can't accept that." The tears spilled over, and her hand gripped his arm. "You have to marry me. I'll be. . .I'll be ruined if you don't."

"Your social set won't bat an eye at the broken engagement. You'll soon land a new victim to work your wiles on. What about that Anthony character your mother mentioned? Why not track him down?"

She swiped at her tears, and her shoulders shook. "I. . .I. . . did. I tried. He just laughed and said I wouldn't trap him into marriage. Sam, I have to get married. . .and soon. Please," she pleaded again. "You've always been so gallant, won't you be gallant now? Save me, save my reputation, please?"

Her desperation suddenly made sense. The whirlwind courtship, the rush to the altar. . . She'd lined him up from the minute he'd said hello. "Who's the father?" Like it mattered.

A sob choked her, but she managed to whisper, "Anthony."

"And the bounder has no intention of marrying you? He knows about the child?" Outrage, not so much for Yvette as for the child, boiled through him. What kind of man walked away from a woman when she was carrying his child?

"He knows. He ran away even faster than you. On the morning train to Chicago."

Sam jammed his hands into his pockets and gritted his teeth. What a mess. He shook his head, rocking on his heels. "You know, I didn't think my pride could be beaten down any further after overhearing you call me a sheep, but I hadn't reckoned on this. Worse than just marrying me for my money, you planned to rush me to the altar so you could pass off your child as mine? We've known each other for almost six weeks. Have you known the whole time that you were carrying? Did you think I wouldn't know? Or that I was so besotted with you that once I found out I wouldn't care? You must think I'm as dumb as a sack of hammers."

Her legs seemed to give way beneath her, and she wobbled. He had to grab her to keep her from collapsing on the floor. Lifting her into his arms, he made for an empty bench.

She wrapped her arms around his neck—a motion that had once sent his heart into orbit—and whispered against his neck, "Please Sam, won't you help me?"

Kneeling, he placed her onto the bench and disengaged her arms. "Yvette, I'm truly sorry for your situation, but I won't marry you." She sobbed into his handkerchief, and he motioned for one of the porters hovering nearby. "Will you get one of the lady porters from the ladies' waiting room?"

Several people stopped and whispered among themselves.

Sam's collar tightened, and he glanced at the wall clock. Less than a quarter of an hour until the train pulled out.

Yvette swung her legs over the edge of the bench. Her shoulders hunched, and she looked small and defenseless, not much like the vivacious, confident woman he'd thought he'd known. "What will I do now? Everything's ruined."

He sighed. "You'll go home to your family and sort this

out. Your mother can have the authorities track this Anthony joker down and make him do right by you. At the very least, you won't be out on the street. You've got money."

Another wail burst through the handkerchief. "But we don't. It's all a sham, don't you see? The house and furniture are rented. At that, we only kept the salon nicely furnished. The rest of the house is bare bones. Mother overdrew her account to see me clothed for the season. If you don't marry me, we'll be out on the street in less than a month."

He hung his head. Christian charity demanded he do something, but what? Not marriage, that was for sure. At the least, he could see she had some money to tide her over. He reached into his inside pocket for his wallet. He frowned. It wasn't there. Then, shaking his head, he remembered tipping the porter outside. He'd slipped his wallet into his coat pocket afterward. But when he checked his coat pocket, he found only lint.

Tracking quickly back through his mind, he remembered the dark-haired urchin who'd bumped into him on the platform. The little rat had stolen his wallet!

❧

"You have your tickets, dear?"

Eldora nodded at the elderly Miss Mackenzie and patted her pocket. "Yes ma'am." She returned her hand to Tick's, whose little face looked pinched. On her other side, Celeste sat primly, her glossy black braids lying just so on her shoulders and her hands folded in her lap. She kept her scarf pulled high, and her beautiful blue eyes missed nothing of the bustle around them. Eldora couldn't help but compare her to an exquisite china doll she'd once seen in a shop window. White skin, thick black lashes, sweet disposition, delicate nose, serene brow. She sighed. Nearly flawless.

"I hope you know I had nothing to do with this. My

strenuous veto was overridden in the board meeting." Miss Mackenzie fussed with her stole. "Those men can be so thickheaded. Mr. Korbin can be particularly trying." Her mouth pinched. "What we need is a few more women on the board of directors. Then we'd see some progress. That's one of the first things I intend to change."

Miss Mackenzie sniffed and dabbed her nose with a lace handkerchief. "I can't believe he just dumped you here. The least Mr. Korbin could've done was to see you onto the train and wait for your departure before running away." She shifted, and the scent of lavender sachets drifted from her beaded dress.

Eldora breathed in. Her mother had used lavender, and the smell took Eldora right back to the time when she had been the doted-on daughter of two happy parents. She shrugged away the memory. "It's all right. I do thank you for waiting with us though. I confess I'm rather nervous being in charge of three children all the way to Denver." Eldora made another conscious effort to loosen her stomach muscles. Every time she stopped thinking about relaxing, the tension returned until her muscles trembled. "I've never done anything like this."

Miss Mackenzie patted Eldora's knee. "You'll do just fine. And I told you, my nephew will be on the train, too. If you run into any trouble, or if you need anything, send for him."

Her nephew, Sam Mackenzie. The nice young man who had given her the box of chocolates. Her imagination brought him instantly to view. His broad shoulders, his trim waist. Sandy-blond hair and tanned skin. And the kindest blue eyes she'd ever seen.

She could almost taste the chocolate caramel on her tongue and hear the excited squeals of the children when she'd shared the bounty. Each piece had been cut in two so there would be enough. For some, it was the first time they'd tasted such a treat, and for others, it brought back memories of better times, before the orphanage. Before oatmeal twice a day and cabbage and salt pork every evening.

"You have the letter to the Denver orphanage?"

Eldora suppressed a smile, knowing all this checking and rechecking was Miss Mackenzie's way of assuring herself they would be fine. "Yes ma'am. Mr. Korbin gave it to me before he left, along with enough money to feed us on the trip." The director had given her multiple warnings not to lose or squander the money. His voice held no confidence she could accomplish the task, something she feared he was correct in. She glanced once more at Celeste and then at Tick. She'd have to be a fool not to know Mr. Korbin was merely ridding himself of four problems, shunting them off to another orphanage because he didn't want to deal with them anymore.

"When are we leaving?" Tick coughed and squirmed. "Will we really sleep on the train?" He coughed again and swiped at his nose with the heel of his hand.

"Sit still, young man." Miss Mackenzie subdued him with a glance. "Children should be seen and not heard."

Tick set his mouth in a mutinous line and stopped his squirming. Eldora patted his bony knee. She'd never subscribed to that old adage, since children often had excellent observations and thoughts to express. Though she believed in kind, respectful speech, she thought it wrong to stifle children in the presence of adults.

She glanced over her shoulder to where Phin was supposed to be watching over their single valise until the call to board. The valise sat alone, unguarded. Eldora drew her hands into fists. "Miss Mackenzie, will you wait here with the children? Phin seems to have wandered off." She rose, not waiting for an answer, and hurried to their bag. Snatching it up, she spun and surveyed the room, looking for his lithe figure and dark hair. The little monster. He'd promised.

She took two steps toward the door marked To TRAINS when a commotion caught her eye. Several people surrounded a redheaded woman on a bench who appeared to be crying. Was she ill? A large woman wearing a porteress's uniform parted the crowd. The waiting passengers seemed to draw a collective sigh at the sight of authority, and they began to disperse.

That's when she spied Phin. He dangled from the grasp of a very angry Sam Mackenzie.

four

Eldora ran across the waiting room, bumping into people and not stopping to apologize. The valise banged against her leg and collided with people in her haste, and she swept it up into her arms to keep from losing it altogether. "Sir, what are you doing?" The words burst from her as she skidded to a stop beside Mr. Mackenzie. "Put that child down."

"Child? Hardly that. He stole my wallet." The man lowered Phin until his feet touched the ground and shifted his grip from the boy's arms to his collar. The man's irate expression softened to surprised recognition. "Say, you're the girl from the orphanage."

While it was pleasant to be remembered, they had more important things to deal with. She turned her attention away from him to confront the boy. "Phin, you promised."

The boy didn't even have the grace to look abashed. He set his jaw and crossed his arms, glaring through his coltish forelock and leaning away from Mr. Mackenzie. "Turkeyhead, picking on a little kid. You gonna beat me, mister? A poor orphan?"

With a shake that made Phin's forelock bounce, Mr. Mackenzie dragged them back toward one of the walls. "Little kid? You've got to be what, thirteen? Beyond old enough to know better. You're fortunate I don't call the authorities to deal with you."

"I ain't scared of you. Call them. I'd rather stay here in jail than get on the train anyway."

Keeping an unrelenting grip on Phin's collar, Mr. Mackenzie

went through the boy's pockets. In the last one, he found his own wallet. The lines alongside his mouth deepened. "I'm of a mind to turn you over and shake you just to make sure that's all you've got on you."

"You don't scare me. I bet the matron could take you out with one whack of her brush." Phin puffed up and took a swing at Mr. Mackenzie, but his arms were too short, and he flailed the air.

"Phin, enough." Eldora wanted to shake the boy herself, though she'd breathed a sigh of relief that the wallet was all Phin had apparently stolen this time. "Please, Mr. Mackenzie, don't call the authorities. I'm so sorry. Phin, apologize to Mr. Mackenzie so we can get on the train."

"Forget it." Phin glared at her. "I'm not going. I can't leave the city. My uncle's coming back for me. He won't be able to find me if I'm in Denver. I'm better off here in jail than hundreds of miles away in another orphanage."

Familiar pain sliced through Eldora. Phin boasted often of his uncle, the one who was coming back any day now to get him. The one who had dropped him off at the orphanage five years before with a promise to return. She turned to Mr. Mackenzie. "Are you going to bring in the police, Mr. Mackenzie?"

His grip eased. "No, there's no time for that. They'll be calling us to the train any minute."

"Hey." Phin stuck out his bottom lip and lowered his brows at Eldora. "How is it you know this big skite?"

The call to trains saved her from having to answer. "We've got to go." She grabbed Phin's hand, though he tried to tug out of her grip.

Mr. Mackenzie released his hold on the boy's collar with a scowl. "I'll be right back. Go over to my aunt, and I'll meet you there and see you on the train." He turned and marched over to the bench where the redheaded woman still sat.

No wonder she'd been crying. Perhaps they were in love and going to be parted for a while. Eldora sighed and shook her head, hearing the matron's admonition to stop her woolgathering daydreams and be practical.

She turned to go back to Tick and Celeste, but Phin dug in his heels. "I told you I'm not going on the train. I'm staying here where Uncle Myatt can find me."

Though slight, Phin was wiry-strong, and Eldora knew she couldn't physically force him to go. But if he didn't go, she couldn't deliver him to the orphanage in Denver. If she failed to deliver all three children to the orphanage, Mr. Korbin would not wire her the money for her return ticket. Desperation thickened her voice. "Phin, please. We left word with Mrs. Scrabeck at the orphanage where you could be found if your uncle should show up. I need you on this trip. I can't do this without you. And what about Tick? If you don't go with us, he'll be all alone. Please, Phin."

Phin's tough expression crumbled a bit around the edges. If he had any weak spot, it was Tick. He rubbed his chin as if considering the situation. "I guess I could at least help you get the kids to Denver. Nothing says I have to stay there. I could hop a return train to St. Louie and be back here before New Year's."

Eldora's knees went wobbly. She gave Phin a trembly smile and let his hand go. "Thank you, Phin. I knew I could count on you."

&

Sam helped Yvette to her feet and escorted her to where Aunt Tabitha sat with two children. He almost laughed at the look on Tabitha's face. Her nose twitched like she'd just smelled something foul but was too polite to mention it. "Yvette, sit here with these children for a moment while

I talk to my aunt."

Tabitha levered herself up and walked with him a few paces. "What did she want?"

Though he was loathe to spill Yvette's secrets to anyone, he needed Tabitha's help in the matter. "She's going to have a baby."

Tabitha jerked as if he'd slapped her, and he put up his hands.

"The child isn't mine."

She relaxed a fraction, but her eyes were wary. "Is there time to tell me the story?"

"Not all of it, but enough. From what I gather, she and her mother are broke, the father of the child has skipped town, and they're about to be evicted from their house. I know it's a lot to ask, and I have no real right to do so, but would you consider helping them out? Investigate her claims, since we both know what a liar she is, but maybe see if you can get them settled in a house somewhere, maybe find a job for Hortense so she can support them?" He dug in his newly reclaimed wallet, happy to see the little thief had left the cash inside. "Give her this." He pressed some bills into Tabitha's hand while the train whistle blew. "I've got to go."

She lifted her wrinkled cheek for his kiss. "I'll look into it. If her claims are true, I'll see what I can do." She folded the bills and tucked them into her bag. "Give my love to the family, and remind your father if he doesn't come visit me soon, he might find me on his doorstep checking up on him."

"I will, and thank you." He squeezed her hand gently in deference to her delicate bones. The young woman from the orphanage approached, her hand on the shoulder of the pickpocket.

"Miss Carter, this is my great-nephew, Sam Mackenzie.

Sam, this is Miss Eldora Carter and her charges. She'll introduce the children once you're on the train."

Eldora. The name seemed too old for her. This entire enterprise seemed too much for someone her age. Wrangling a petty thief would be bad enough, but she had two others to manage as well. "Let me take your bag for you."

The older boy—Phin, she'd called him?—snatched the battered valise and glared at Sam. "I can get it."

"Fine." If the boy had his hands full, he couldn't be dipping them into others' pockets. "Shall we?" He took Eldora's elbow. The little boy slid off the bench and took her hand on the other side, and the girl stood up gracefully and adjusted her scarf. She'd be about ten, he supposed, though guessing little girls' ages wasn't something at which he was proficient. Why had no one adopted such a strikingly beautiful child?

"Are we going to the train now?" The small boy might be six or seven. He had a sort of stretched-tight, worn-thin look about him, though he almost quivered with excitement. Maybe a little mountain air and some good food would brace him up, make him a little more robust.

Yvette shot him one last pleading glance, and he had the feeling of wriggling out of a trap as he walked away from her. He'd done the best he could short of marrying her, and that he was not prepared to do.

He held the door for Miss Carter and the kids and ushered them outside, casting a thank you over his shoulder to Aunt Tabitha.

She nodded and joined Yvette on the bench, making a shooing motion toward Sam.

The conductor was picking up his stepstool when they reached the edge of the platform. "Just in time." He replaced the wooden box and offered his hand to Miss Carter, then swung the girl after her.

The little boy scrambled up, followed by Phin and the bag.

The conductor consulted his watch. "You can board here and walk through two cars to get to your private car, Mr. Mackenzie."

Sam nodded and grasped the cold, metal handrail. He'd just see them settled and head to the privacy and peace of the Mackenzie private car. Yvette's condition had shocked him more than he cared to admit, and he needed a little time to sort things out in his mind.

The conductor pointed to the overhead rack tilted out from the wall. "You can stow your bag there or under the seat." He checked his watch again as the train whistle blasted. "You might want to take your seats. We'll be pulling out any minute now." He continued up the car, nodding to passengers, stopping to talk to some.

Two velvet-covered benches facing each other defined a seating area. The smaller boy hopped up to kneel next to the window, his thin face alive with excitement. Phin shoved his hair out of his eyes and tossed the valise under their seat. Eldora ushered the girl ahead of herself. She looked so fragile and uncertain, as wide-eyed as the kids, though she was supposed to be in charge.

"You'll be fine here, right? If you need anything, ask the conductor or have him send someone to my car at the rear of the train." The train lurched, and Sam grabbed the back of a bench. Somehow it felt wrong to just abandon her here, but what else was he supposed to do? His instructions from Tabitha were to see her and the kids onto the train and maybe check in on them occasionally to make sure they were doing all right. Odd to feel this conflicted over leaving her when leaving Yvette had brought only relief. He shook his head. Addlepated, that's what he was.

"We'll be fine. Thank you for seeing us onto the train."

"I won't be far away if you need me. You've got your tickets, right?"

She nodded, patting her pocket. "Your aunt asked me several times."

"All right. I'm going to go now." He turned to Phin. "Behave yourself and watch out for the ladies."

Phin glared back and said nothing.

The smaller boy bounced on the seat, his feet knocking into Phin's leg. "We're moving, Phin. Lookit how fast!" He pointed to the buildings sliding past the window as the train gained momentum. If he was this thrilled by train-yard speed, what would he be like once they got onto the open prairie?

"Tickets, please." The conductor approached, stopping at each set of seats. Sam shifted his weight and decided to remain just long enough to be sure she had the tickets properly punched. When the conductor drew near, Eldora dug in her pocket and produced the pasteboards. Her eyes seemed to swallow up her face, liquid pools the color of caramels, and a tremulous smile touched her lips when she looked up.

While the conductor worked his hole punch, Phin swatted the thin boy's feet off the bench. "Turn around and sit down, Tick. There's no room for your boots up here." He tugged his cloth cap down and folded his arms as if preparing for a snooze.

Eyes narrowed, the smaller child snatched the cap and tossed it onto the floor.

Phin jolted upright and snarled. "Tick, you rat. Pick that up!" He grabbed the boy's wrist and forced it down toward the floor.

Tick squirmed out of Phin's grasp and tripped over his feet, sprawling into the aisle. He popped up and whirled to face the bigger boy. "You're acting like you think this ain't no big deal, but I know better. You ain't never been on a train before. You ain't never been out of the city." He plowed into Phin, elbows jutting, puny fists swinging. "Admit it, you're excited and maybe even a little scared."

In their jostling, they tumbled into the space between the seats and rammed into Eldora and the little girl.

"Phin, Tick, stop it this instant!" Eldora tried to grab a flailing arm as the boys tussled but got an elbow in the chin for her trouble. She rocked back blinking.

Heads turned. The conductor started back their way. "I say, miss, you must control these children. We can't have them brawling in the middle of the car."

Phin struck out and his boot connected with the conductor's shin. The squabble had the attention of everyone in the car.

"Boys, knock it off." Sam reached into the fray, grabbing whatever appendage he could. Little hooligans. He wound up with Phin's wrist and Tick's ankle. Righting the little boy, he pushed both of them back into their seats. In his efforts to get them off the floor and separated, his arm brushed the girl, snagging her scarf and dragging it off. He glanced up to beg her pardon and froze. A quiver rippled through him, and he couldn't look away.

Below the china-blue eyes and perfect porcelain skin, her mouth was a ravaged mess. Where her upper lip should have been, a gaping hole snarled, the edges disappearing into her right nostril. Her teeth jutted at odd angles in the opening. She grabbed the muffler and tried to put it up before anyone else saw, but it was too late.

A woman let out a shriek, and a man gasped.

"Lookit that!" A boy nearly Phin's age hung over the seat ahead of them and pointed. "What a freak!" He doubled over with laughter, and before Sam could prevent it, Phin punched the jeering boy right in the mouth.

five

Sam had a fraction of a second to shoot an arrow of prayer for patience heavenward before braving the fray.

Phin launched himself over the back of the seat and pinned the boy. Tick followed suit, shouting, "Stop your laughing, you skunk. I'll beat you to a powder."

Even as Sam hauled both boys off the offender, he marveled at their swift change from foes to allies. Evidently they could beat on each other all they wanted, but nobody from outside was allowed to without consequences.

"Ha, now you've got a split lip, dog face!" Tick took one last weak swing, his face pasty white and his little ribcage working like a bellows. A bluish tinge colored his lips.

The conductor's genial expression fused into a hard mask. "Miss, we cannot allow this kind of behavior on the train. You'll have to control the boys, or they will have to be put off at the next stop." He darted a glance at the little girl who had tugged her scarf over her face once more and whose eyes now brimmed with tears.

Eldora put her arm around the child and drew her into her side. "Sir, please, I am sorry. I'll make them behave. Don't put us off, please. We'll try not to trouble you or anyone else."

It bothered Sam that she should be apologizing for the boys when they should be apologizing for themselves, and that the conductor had nothing to say about the poor manners of the people who gawked and jeered at a little girl with a deformed face. Before he could speak, one of those ill-mannered passengers voiced her opinion.

"Those little hoodlums should be in jail, and that girl should be in an asylum. What's she doing out among decent people with a face like that?" A woman's high-pitched inquiry shot through the car. She hoisted her ample self up and leaned over the seat to glare at the little girl as if everything was somehow the child's fault. "I've never seen anything so awful in all my life. What is the railroad thinking putting brawling children and deformed freaks in with the regular passengers?"

Phin stiffened and then bolted out of his seat. "You fat old sow! Your sour face is worse than a harelip. Celeste can't help her twisted mouth, but you sneer on purpose. Your nasty mug would curdle fresh milk."

"Phin!" Eldora's chin dropped, and she stood.

Sam—though he wanted to cheer and second the boy's opinion—clapped his hand over Phin's mouth and dragged him backward before he could launch himself at the woman. How had a simple errand for his aunt turned into this debacle? They hadn't been on the train ten minutes yet, and already the entire complement of passengers wanted them off. "Enough, Phin." He spun the boy toward the door they'd entered by and gave him a push. "March."

The boy scowled over his shoulder and barely caught the valise Sam tossed at him. Sam sent Tick after Phin, scooped the tearful Celeste onto his arm, and grabbed Eldora by the elbow.

The conductor barred their way. "Sir, where are you going? The next car is full. This is the only passenger car with any room left. I don't have anywhere else for them to go."

"Fortunately, I do." Sam guided Eldora to the door and then turned to face the length of the car. "You all should be ashamed of yourselves, driving these orphaned kids away. I apologize for the fracas, but in one thing Phin was right." He leveled a stare at the woman who had been so rude. "These kids are what they are through no choice of their own. But you all here had a choice as to how you would accept them, and you chose badly." His little group clustered near the door, and he took Eldora's elbow again.

"Where are you taking us?" She sounded like she was being strangled. "You heard the conductor. There's no room for us in the next car."

"Just keep walking." He hitched Celeste higher on his arm and opened the door to the platform. Cold air rushed at him, and the noise of wheels on rails deafened speech. Keeping a good hold on each of them, he transferred them one at a time to the next platform and through the crowded car.

The little boy held his chest, wheezing. Without being asked, Phin handed the valise to Eldora and lifted Tick up.

"I'm not a baby," Tick protested weakly.

"Hush up. You're about done in. Fighting takes it out of a man." Phin shoved the boy's head down on his shoulder and looked to Sam for what to do next.

"Please, Mr. Mackenzie, where are you taking us?" Eldora stopped at the end of the car and faced Sam like a prisoner before a firing squad.

"My private car at the end of the train. There's plenty of room and no one to complain about the children." He opened the door and moved them across to the railed platform at the end of the Mackenzie car. Using his key, he unlocked the door and stepped aside for them all to enter.

Warmth surrounded them, and when he closed the door behind him, the noise lowered. He eased Celeste down onto the closest chair, and Phin did the same for Tick.

Eldora stood in the middle of the salon, clutching the threadbare valise and staring at the rich pecan woodwork, etched mirrors, and gilded metalwork. Her pink lips parted. "Oh my."

Phin let out a low whistle. "Pretty swank. You must be loaded. Who'd you rob to get this palace on wheels?" He ran his hand along the carved back of the chair Tick sagged on.

Sam sighed. "I didn't rob anyone. My family and I own some silver mines in Colorado."

Eldora dropped the valise and half-turned to stare at him. "You're a miner? A mine owner?"

"Yes, Mackenzie Mining Company." He frowned when she shot him an accusatory glare. "Is there something wrong with that?"

&

Eldora had a moment to imagine her knight in shining armor toppling off his white charger into a clanking pile in the dust. A miner. Not just a miner, but a mine owner. "No, there's nothing wrong with that."

Except that even a poor orphan like her had heard of the Mackenzie Mining Company. He was one of *those* Mackenzies. So far above and beyond anything Eldora could aspire to, it made her cringe. Here they'd been wallowing and brawling in front of him, and now they'd imposed themselves on him like beggars.

A cold wind blew through her, though she stood beside a coal stove, cherry-red with warmth. "Tick, are you all right?" She knelt beside him and touched his cheek.

He opened his eyes and nodded. "Peachy. Just need to catch my breath." He put his hand against his chest and his ribs pumped.

"Lie still for a while." She shrugged out of her shawl and tucked it around him. He looked as if a puff of air would blow him away. Her stomach tightened. The only instructions she'd been given regarding Tick were about keeping him calm and warm. So far she was zero for two.

"Is his name really Tick?" Mr. Mackenzie raised the glass

on one of the wall sconces and lit the lamp, bringing more light into the elegant salon.

Eldora smoothed the boy's light-as-air white hair onto his forehead. "No, his name is Michael. But he sticks so close to Phin, the kids started calling him Tick. Now that's all he'll answer to. Isn't that right, Tick?"

"Me 'n Phin stick together." He puffed up a little and threw a smug look Phin's way.

Phin jerked his chin in agreement.

"Tick arrived on the orphanage doorstep about the same time as Phin. They've been fast friends ever since, though as you saw in the other car they tend to squabble quite a bit."

Mr. Mackenzie nodded and squatted beside her. "Like brothers. My older brother and I have been known to mix it up from time to time." He scrutinized Tick, his brows drawn together.

Eldora glanced at Celeste. Her scarf once again covered the lower half of her face, and she sat perfectly still, feet primly together, hands in her lap, staring at the floor. Everything about her posture begged no one to notice her, and all trace of tears had subsided. She looked controlled and composed. That bothered Eldora. Celeste was too controlled. She should be crying right now, angry and hurt. Instead, because she was accustomed to the cruelty of others, she withdrew even deeper into herself.

"This is Celeste. She's ten." Eldora rose and put her hand on Celeste's shoulder.

The little girl tilted her head and flicked her lashes upward for a quick peek at Eldora's face, then returned to staring at the floor.

"Pleased to make your acquaintance, Celeste." Still squatting, he patted Celeste's knee and then pushed himself upright. Eldora liked the way his voice softened when he spoke to the little girl. "And you're Phin."

"Phineas Bartholomew, at your service." Phin removed his flat cloth cap and bowed low. When he straightened, he swept aside his black forelock and grinned. The smile was not returned.

"Let me have your bag. Leave the children here, and I'll show you where everything is." He turned to Phin. "Keep your hands in your pockets, and stay in this room. Got it?"

"Who died and made you emperor? I won't nick anything while you're gone." Phin made a show of jamming his hands into his pockets.

Why did he always have to choose the hard way to do everything? Couldn't he see how much they were already beholden to Mr. Mackenzie? Eldora sent him a half-imploring, half-exasperated look and followed their host.

He stopped at the first door in the narrow passageway. "I hope you don't mind sharing a room with the little girl." A match *scritched* and flared as he lit a kerosene lamp beside the door. "When we travel, this is my parents' room." A double bed with an indigo satin spread took up most of the space. "The water closet is next door." He indicated a narrow door into a well-appointed washroom.

A porcelain sink stood in one corner, and a zinc-lined tub peeped from behind a curtain. A whole washroom all to themselves. The image of the ranks of sinks and commodes in the orphanage community washroom came to her mind. "We won't mind sharing. We're used to it." Eldora hadn't had a room of her own since she first came to the orphanage. To share a room with only one other girl would be a luxury.

In the next compartment, two chairs sat facing one another. He lit another lamp. "The boys can stay in here. The chairs fold out into a bed, and another bunk lowers from up there, Pullman-style." He pointed to a brass handle set into the sloping wall above her head.

The paneling gleamed, and everything screamed money and privilege. Even more than the upscale houses where she had been a domestic, this railcar bespoke the wealth and power behind the man so casually showing her about.

He sauntered toward the rear of the car, past a narrow galley, cold and dark, and another bedroom—his own?—and on to another salon, this one doubling as a dining room with a table and chairs in one corner and sofas lining the other walls. Olive-green velvet drapes with gold fringe trim hung from every window, and stained glass transoms defined the overhead space.

"What kind of mining does your company do?"

He shrugged. "Silver mostly. And lead."

She pressed her hand to her middle. At least it wasn't coal. But did that change anything? No. He still sent men down into the bowels of the earth to bring him treasure. And sometimes those men didn't return. Men like her father.

"The kitchen isn't in use on this trip. I had figured to eat in the dining car with the other passengers, but I can see that won't be possible now. I'll talk to the conductor in the morning about having trays sent in. Let's get back to the children."

He waited for her to precede him up the passageway, something men in her experience rarely did for girls like her. Kindness and consideration marked everything he did. Did those practices extend to his mine workers? And why did she care so much?

Phin stood exactly where they had left him, hands still in his pockets. When she entered the room, he withdrew his hands and flopped onto the settee. "Didn't steal a thing—this time."

"Phin, that's enough." Eldora rounded on him. "We're

beholden to Mr. Mackenzie for too many things for you to be so churlish." She wanted to press her fists to her temples and give in to the overwhelming sense of drowning in the responsibilities heaped on her.

"Call me Sam. You're not beholden to me. I'm doing this as a favor to my aunt. She asked me to look after you."

The little knife that had been thrust into her heart when she learned he was a mine owner twisted a half-turn. All his kindness was merely a favor for his aunt. Eldora sagged onto the sofa and chided her reflection in the dark window across the car. She'd been silly to spin daydreams. Her would-be hero had feet of clay.

six

Sam awoke to a strong knock on the door. A quick peek through bleary eyes showed no light coming around the window blinds. "Who is it?"

"Mr. Mackenzie, it's the conductor. I apologize for entering your car unannounced, but I need a word with you."

"Can't it wait till morning?" He wanted to stuff his head back under his pillows. Morning wasn't his favorite time, and he liked dead-of-night-before-morning even less.

"I'm afraid not. It concerns one of your charges."

For a moment, he thought the conductor was talking about the dynamite used in the mines. "Charges?"

"One of the children, sir."

Remembrance rushed back to him. The kids. And Eldora Carter. He swung his feet over the side of the bed and scrubbed his hands through his hair. A yawn threatened to crack his jaw. "I'll be out in a minute."

"Very good, sir. I'll meet you in the salon."

Stumbling into his clothes, yawning every few seconds, he managed to drag himself to the end of the railcar. He hadn't bothered to button his shirt all the way nor to find socks and boots. Since he could barely keep his eyes open, he planned to deal with whatever the problem was and then fall back into his bed until daylight.

The conductor—every shiny brass button secured through its corresponding buttonhole—stood in the center of the room.

Phin stood with his back to the wall, hands behind him,

49

chin tucked low, glaring out of the tops of his eyes. "I told you, I didn't steal your watch." The boy's face paled, and his thin chest rose and fell under his threadbare shirt and jacket.

Sam groaned and scratched the stubble on his jaw. "Is that what this is about? Give it back, Phin. I told you to lay off the stealing."

Lifting his chin, Phin braced his legs so hard his muscles quivered, but his hands remained behind his back. "I said I didn't take it."

Rolling his shoulders, stiff from the strange bed, Sam yawned again. "You'll have to forgive my doubts since you managed to light-finger my wallet just yesterday. What are you doing wandering the train in the middle of the night?"

Phin snorted. "It ain't the middle of the night. It's getting on for five o'clock. Or do you rich gents sleep till noon every day? Matron would've kicked you out of your cot a half-hour since if you were at the orphanage."

His sneer grated Sam's skin. As soon as he got the sand out of his eyes, he was going to clobber the little snot. "What're you hiding then if not the watch?"

"None of your affair."

Sam decided he'd had enough. "I'm giving you fair warning. I'm a man to be reckoned with, especially on short sleep. Hand over whatever it is so I can go back to bed, or I'll have to take it from you."

The conductor advanced on Phin. "The truth is I had my watch before I found you in the dining car bothering the attendants, and now my watch is missing. The head waiter told me you were bragging about your pickpocket abilities, and you ran the moment you knew I was looking for you."

Red suffused Phin's high cheekbones. His dark eyes glittered in the candlelight, and his lips set in a thin line. Withdrawing his hand, he opened his fingers to reveal a squashed hunk of bread. "That's all I took."

"I insist we search his pockets." The conductor grabbed Phin by the arm when someone pounded on the door.

"Hold up there." Sam sauntered to the door. "Might as well be back in the St. Louis railway station, what with all the coming and going." He opened the door, letting in a gust of cold air along with a white-coated waiter.

"Suh, you were missing your watch? We found it on your breakfast table." He dangled the golden timepiece from its chain.

"I told you I didn't take your stupid old watch!" Phin reared back and hurled the chunk of bread at the conductor. The crust bounced off the man's wire-rimmed glasses.

Sam lunged for the boy before he could follow the bread with his fist.

"Lemme go!"

"Calm down." Sam had his hands full with the wiry boy. "Stop it!" He pinned Phin's arms.

"What's going on here?" Eldora's question sliced through the air, freezing everyone for a second.

Sam whirled, dragging Phin around with him.

Barefooted, gripping a shawl around her slender shoulders, and with her hair in a wispy braid, Eldora looked about fifteen. "Sam, what are you doing to him?"

Celeste peeped around the corner, her mouth hidden by her hands.

Phin took up his struggling again. "He's hurting me. He's going to throw me off the train." His accusations flew like his wiry arms.

"No!" A tow-headed bullet in a short nightshirt launched itself across the room and barreled into Sam's knees. "Let him go! Let him go!" Tiny fists pummeled his leg. Tick butted him and then looked up, blue eyes swimming with tears. He blinked and the tears spilled over; then he backed up and wobbled a couple steps. His face was pale as milk, and his lips gasped like a fish in the bottom of a rowboat. Without a sound, he collapsed onto the carpet.

Sam's arms went limp, and Phin sprang from his grasp.

With a cry, Eldora dropped beside Tick and patted his face.

Phin shoved her aside and straddled Tick. He pressed his ear to Tick's chest. "Nothing!" Before anyone could stop him, he lifted his hand into a fist over his head then dropped it sharply, punching Tick in the chest.

❧

Eldora rocked back when Phin shoved her, and she cracked her shoulder against the wall. A cry burst from her lips, both from the pain and from the shock of seeing Phin hit Tick so hard.

The small boy's body jerked, and Phin thrust his ear down to listen to Tick's chest once again.

Her legs tangled in the hem of her nightgown, and she grappled with her shawl, her braid, and the rocking of the train.

The three men in the room seemed frozen in place, jaws slack, eyebrows high.

She lunged forward to push Phin off Tick, but he evaded her unsteady attempt, keeping his attention focused on the little boy. A lump lodged in her throat, and her heart raced faster than the train. Tick!

"C'mon, Tick!" Phin pounded the boy's chest again. "C'mon!" He jammed his ear against Tick's ribs. Eldora's fright was mirrored in Phin's dark eyes.

Sam seemed to come unstuck from the floor and in two strides crossed the salon to haul Phin upright.

Phin dangled from his grasp, writhing. "No! Lemme go! Lemme go!"

Eldora bent over Tick, noting his blue lips and his eyes rolled back in his head.

Phin shrugged out of his jacket and pounced on Tick once more. He slammed into Tick's chest.

The little boy jolted and took a staggering breath. His eyelids fluttered open, and his glassy eyes tried to focus on her face. He groaned, the sweetest sound Eldora had ever heard, and dragged his hand to his chest.

Sam hauled Phin off again, grunting with the effort.

At Tick's movements, Phin went limp in Sam's grip and blew out a long sigh.

Sam shook Phin. "What do you mean, jumping on him that way? Ellie, is he all right?"

Even in her befuddled state, it registered that Sam had called her Ellie. She'd have to take that out and ponder it later. Gathering Tick in her arms, she stroked his hair and hugged him.

He sank against her, his chest rising and falling rapidly. "What happened?" His voice sounded thin as paper.

"You dropped to the floor, and—" She stopped. "I'm not exactly sure what happened—it all happened so fast."

The conductor advanced on Phin and, shoving his hands against Phin's shoulders, pinned him to the wall. "That boy is a menace! First fighting in the passenger car, then stealing food, and by your own admission"—he pointed to Sam—"your wallet, and now pummeling a defenseless child in the throes of some kind of fit. I won't have him on my train, under your protection or not, Mr. Mackenzie."

The white-coated waiter hovered near the door, the whites of his eyes a stark contrast to his dark face. He stood still, as if charmed like a rabbit watching a rattlesnake, his hand clutching the doorknob.

Sam interposed himself between the conductor and Phin.

His eyes snapped fire, and his muscular frame, barefooted and with shirt hanging half open, dwarfed the railroad official. "That will be all. I'll get to the bottom of everything here, and I can assure you Phin will be no more trouble."

Eldora averted her eyes when she realized she was staring at Sam's half-bare chest. Heat bloomed in her cheeks, for she had never seen a man so carelessly attired. That same heat warmed her heart, for he was championing Phin. She took herself severely to task.

Don't go getting any romantic notions about him, or any man, Eldora Carter. Just because he's being kind in taking up for you and the children doesn't mean anything. A plain-as-potatoes orphan wouldn't attract the attention of someone as wealthy and handsome as Sam Mackenzie.

The conductor raised himself to his full height—still several inches shorter than Sam—and puffed out his chest. "If there is one more incident regarding that boy before this train reaches Denver, I'll put him off, even if I have to stop in the middle of the prairie to do so."

Phin leaned around Sam and bared his teeth, giving the conductor what the orphans referred to as "the stink eye." Phin had always proven quite adept at this expression, turning it on the matron at every opportunity.

Eldora lowered her eyebrows and shook her head at him, giving him her best don't-poke-the-bear expression.

The conductor blinked, turned on his heel, and snatched the watch still dangling from the waiter's hand. He all but shoved the staff-man ahead of him out onto the platform and slammed the door so hard the windows rattled.

Celeste nudged her arm, giving her a fright. "Yes?" Eldora managed.

The little girl leaned in close and whispered as she always did, afraid someone would hear her garbled speech and poke fun. "Don't be mad at Thfin. He did that wunth before and Thickth heart stharted again."

Eldora nodded and flicked a reassuring smile at Celeste.

The girl retreated to the passageway once more, tugging the neckline of her nightgown up just under her nose.

Sam squatted beside Eldora and peered at Tick. Her heart quickened again to have him so near. His hair stood up, and a fine dusting of reddish-blond whiskers covered his cheeks. She forced herself to concentrate on the boy in her arms.

Sam touched Tick's hand. "How you doing, buddy?"

"Fine. I'm sorry I jumped you. I thought you were hurting Phin. Then everything got black around the edges, and I was gone."

Phin elbowed his way in. "Sorry I had to knock you like that. You dropped like a prizefighter with a glass jaw, just like last time."

Eldora shivered, realizing how close they had come to losing Tick. She hugged him harder until he squirmed. She loosened her hold and realized Sam was staring at her.

"What was the orphanage thinking to send you out with these three? You're barely more than a child yourself." His blue eyes had the same softness as when he'd first seen Celeste.

Bitterness coated Eldora's tongue. Charity. Pity. Benevolent largesse on which they must depend forever to survive. Her spine stiffened, and her jaw tightened. "I'm not a child. I'm twenty years old." A thrust of honesty pierced her. "Or I will be this spring." She helped Tick to stand and pushed herself off the floor, righting her shawl and swinging her braid over her shoulder. "Someone has to take care of these children. Who better than me, who knows what it is like to go through life alone, forced to live on the charity of others?"

He blinked and stepped back.

She wanted to recall her harsh tone. Another shiver raced

up her spine. What would they do if he decided to abandon them to the mercies of the passenger car?

He glanced out the window while he buttoned his shirt. "You're going to catch cold standing there in your night things. Everybody get dressed, and I'll see about rustling us up some food." He turned to Phin. "You will not leave this car, is that understood? If the conductor catches you pilfering anything, he'll make good his threat. He's like the captain of a ship. His word is law on this train. In fact, you've antagonized him to the point that he won't have to catch you stealing. He's liable to chuck you off if he so much as catches sight of you."

Phin shoved his hands in his pockets and nodded, staring at the far wall as if he didn't care one way or the other.

Eldora sighed and, with her hand on Tick's shoulder, directed Phin down the passageway to get dressed.

When they reassembled in the salon, breakfast had been laid on the side table. Eldora insisted Tick lay on the settee, and it alarmed her that he acquiesced without complaint. His face was still pale, and his movements a bit shaky. She tucked a rug around him. "Do you want something to eat?" Her brow puckered as his eyelids fluttered closed.

"No. I'm not hungry." His face went lax, and she scrabbled for his wrist to check his pulse. Concern hovered, though she could feel the rapid beats. Tick was always hungry.

She turned back to the table as Sam finished stoking the coal stove and held her chair for her. She wasn't quite sure what to do, since no man had held a chair for her before, but she managed to sit safely and spread her napkin in her lap.

"How is he?" Sam took his seat and glanced over at Tick.

"Sleeping."

"He sure scared me, dropping down like that. I thought he was dead."

Phin barely waited for grace to be said before diving into the food.

Celeste sat primly at the table and ate nothing.

Sam frowned. "Why doesn't she eat something? I thought all kids liked biscuits with jam."

Eldora's eyes caressed the little girl. "You may take your plate to our room if you like, Celeste."

Celeste shot her a grateful glance and picked up her plate and cutlery.

"Can you manage?"

Her black curls bobbed, and she disappeared down the hall.

When she was out of earshot, Eldora explained. "She doesn't like to eat in front of other people. With her mouth the way it is, eating isn't a pretty sight. The kids at the orphanage made terrible fun of her until the matron finally consented to let her eat alone."

"Poor kid. I wish there was something to be done for her." Sam tilted the gravy boat over his biscuits. "Phin, you should slow down and chew that food. It would be better if you actually tasted it before swallowing."

Phin looked up, his cheeks bulging like a gopher's. He swallowed a couple times. "I ain't never had nothing but oatmeal for breakfast for about as long as I can remember. Biscuits and jam, gravy, eggs, sausages. . .do you eat like this every day?"

Eldora could identify with his wonder. She was a bit taken aback by the spread herself, though working as a domestic had shown her some of the world beyond the orphanage.

Sam shrugged. "I guess this is a pretty typical breakfast for me."

"It's a wonder you ain't as round as a beetroot eating like this every day." Phin shoved another spoonful of eggs into his mouth.

Eldora choked and grabbed for her napkin. "Phin, how is it you knew what to do when Tick's heart quit?" She hoped to change the subject before Sam's thundercloud expression broke into a storm all over Phin.

The boy shrugged. "I asked the best doctor in St. Louis about Tick's condition."

"How did you talk to the best doctor in St. Louis?"

"I slipped out of the orphanage one day and asked around for the name of the best doctor in the city. Then I waited by his gate until he came out, and I followed him downtown. Wasn't hard to lift his wallet off him on the street."

Eldora groaned, and Sam's hand tightened on his fork.

"Then I followed him back to his house and returned the wallet—made out like I found it on the street—and he invited me in." Phin waved his fork at the interior of the train car. "His place was nearly as fancy as what you got here. Anyway, I told him I had a friend with some heart trouble and would he mind if I asked him a few questions. He asked all about Tick and told me about thumping him in the chest if he ever dropped down and I couldn't find a heartbeat. He said Tick needed some medicine, but I told him we couldn't afford it. Then I hustled out of there because it was getting late and I knew I was already in for a beating with the radiator brush when I got back anyway."

Sam laid down his fork and knife and sat back, staring at Phin. Finally he shrugged. "What were you doing in the dining car this morning?"

Phin stopped chewing, his eyes growing wary.

A tickle of unease feathered under Eldora's breastbone. With Phin you never knew what he might have been up to. She gripped her napkin in her lap.

"I didn't know if we'd get breakfast this morning, so I snitched some bread for Celeste and Tick. Figured me and

Eldora could go hungry, but the little kids needed something to eat."

Tears pricked Eldora's eyes.

Sam cleared his throat and passed Phin the basket of biscuits.

seven

Eldora throttled the handle of her valise as if trying to squeeze the life out of it, numb to the continual rocking and swaying, the clacking and clatter of the train. The falling dusk through the windows revealed the same sodden, flat landscape they had seen for miles.

Tick still slept on the settee beside her as he had all day, rousing every once in a while to drink some broth and give her a smile that was a mere shadow of its usual self. Celeste turned the pages of a *Harper's Magazine* Sam had dug up somewhere for her, and Phin sprawled in a chair, flipping a poker chip he always had on him, making it walk across the backs of his fingers and appear and disappear. Had to keep his fingers nimble, he claimed.

"Salina! Next stop!" The conductor's voice came through the door, still with a cranky edge.

She supposed she couldn't blame him, being subjected to life with Phin, but the boy hadn't budged from the railcar all day. By now the conductor should be over such things.

"Salina!"

Salina, Kansas. Sam had announced after breakfast they would be stopping over there. "I pressed the conductor pretty hard, and he finally said the best doctor between Topeka and Denver was in Salina. Tick should be under a doctor's care. We'll stop there, and you can get him looked at."

His grave expression pressed Eldora's heart until guilt seeped into every corner. Defensive words flew out. "I'm doing the best I can. I know he needs a doctor, but I can't afford one. I have no money for doctors or medicines or staying over in a strange town. I have to get the children to Denver. Maybe they'll have a doctor there who can treat him."

"Tick never should've left St. Louis, as delicate as he is. Didn't the orphanage have a doctor?"

Phin sat up. "No doctors. Sometimes we'd get a dose of castor oil or the like, but I never saw no doctor there. Wouldn't surprise me a bit if old Korbin wasn't skimming the donations and pocketing the cash himself. Be easy enough to do, if nobody was checking up on him."

Eldora shook her head and frowned. "Phin, that's a thoroughly scurrilous remark. You have no proof Mr. Korbin was embezzling funds."

Phin cocked his head to the side and appraised her. "You always talk like you swallowed a dictionary whenever you're mad at me. Why don't you just say things plain?"

"Fine. I'll give it to you plain. Stop talking about things you know nothing about. Keep your mouth shut, and do as you're told." Eldora regretted her sharp tone the instant the words flew out of her mouth. Here she was, scared to death to be dumped in a strange town with no money or means, and she was taking it out on Phin, who was probably not so far off the mark with his assessment of Mr. Korbin's financial finagling.

Sam rose and shrugged into his coat. "I'll be back in a bit." He shot one warning glance at Phin and slipped out the door.

Eldora fretted the entire time he was gone. The little bit of money Mr. Korbin had given her wouldn't last a day, much less cover an expensive doctor's visit. She had nothing of value to sell to gain the funds. Her only recourse lay in spending the coins to send a wire to the orphanage asking for more money. And what would she do if they denied her request? The train would be gone, she would have no money, and they would have to wait two days for the next train before continuing their journey. At least their tickets to Denver would still be good, but how would she feed the children in the meantime, and what about Tick? Sam was right when he said Tick needed a doctor, but right or not, Sam's words wounded Eldora. She was doing the best she could. She'd like to see him do better in her place.

Sam breezed through the door, shaking droplets of water off his coat and hat. "Salina coming up. Are you all packed?"

She couldn't really blame him for wanting to be rid of them. In only twenty-four hours she and the children had erupted into his life like a firework. He'd been involved in several unpleasant scenes and been forced to share his private car. His quiet return home had turned into a traveling circus. "I've got everything." And precious little it was, too. Skimpy, well-worn night clothes for each of them, and an extra pair of stockings for her and Celeste. At least she could clothe Tick in two nightshirts, since Phin scorned nightwear, preferring to sleep in his pants and shirt. They would be indescribably filthy by the time they reached Denver, if they ever did. Eldora was beginning to despair of arriving there with all three children.

The train jerked to a stop in the rail yard.

"I want to thank you for taking care of the children and me. I know we've put you to considerable trouble." She rose. "You've been most kind. I hope you have more pleasant travels on the remainder of your journey." Though she kept her voice calm, panic thrust against her windpipe and accelerated her heart. Cold rain splattered the windows. How was she going to get Tick off the train? Celeste would have to carry the valise, and she and Phin could trade off carrying the boy. Though she hated to ask for anything more, she forced herself, for Tick's sake, to say the words. "Would it be too much to ask if we could take one of the blankets with us? Tick's coat is less than adequate, and I need to keep him warm and dry." Not to mention if they had to spend the night holed up somewhere in a barn or alley, they could all huddle under it.

Sam's eyebrows rose, and he used his thumb to push back his hat. Water droplets dotted the shoulders of his sheepskin-lined jacket and glistened on his ruddy cheeks. "A blanket? Of course he can keep the blanket. What are you talking about? You don't think I'm just going to toss you off at the depot and go on ahead without you?" His raised eyebrows darted down, and his expression darkened. "What kind of man do you take me for? Leaving a penniless girl and three kids to fend for themselves." He stuck his hands on his waist and glared at her. "Give Phin that bag, and take Celeste's hand. I'll carry the boy. We're all heading into town. I've arranged for the railcar to be put into a siding."

"But, Mr. Mackenzie, I can't—"

"Don't you think we've gotten beyond formal names? I answer to Sam." He stooped and lifted Tick into his arms. "Make sure he's well covered."

Eldora adjusted the blankets, buffaloed by his commanding manner. She should protest that they couldn't take advantage of his generosity any more, that he'd done enough already, but his set jaw and forbidding stare kept her quiet. She took up the valise and Celeste's hand and nodded to Phin to follow Sam out onto the platform.

"You don't have to do what he says, you know. I can take care of us without him." Phin's dark eyes narrowed, the black lashes almost touching.

Eldora shook her head. "We have to think of what's best

for Tick. He needs a doctor. We should be thanking Mr. Mackenzie, not resenting his provision."

"You can thank him all you want, but you wait and see. He'll get tired of playing 'pat-the-head-of-the-poor-orphan' and he'll scamper. Then it will be just us again."

Though she didn't want to agree, she knew from experience that people often tired of good works long before the need for them ended. Benefactors started out on fire, well-intentioned and full of enthusiasm, volunteering and donating. But as soon as anyone started counting on them, they tired of their charitable works and moved on, leaving in their wake needy hearts that grew wary of trusting.

Her thoughts pushed at her like the stiff wind as they left the depot and walked up the street. Phin took the valise and tugged his cloth cap down tight. Celeste anchored her scarf over her face and leaned into the gale. Rain gusted and pelted them, first from one direction and then another. Sam kept his head bent, checking over his shoulder every few moments.

At last they reached the front porch of a brick building. A sign instructed them to enter and walk upstairs to the doctor's office. The quiet calm of the entryway made Eldora's ears ring. She let go of Celeste's hand, and with chilled fingers, she swiped at the raindrops on her cheeks.

"This way. Hope the doc's in." Sam's boots thumped on the treads, and they all followed him. Tick didn't stir, his face tucked into Sam's shoulder. At the top of the stairs, Sam stepped back to allow Eldora to precede him into the office.

The smell of carbolic and licorice wrapped around them, along with the starchy smell of cotton and the tang of vinegar. Eldora guided Celeste to the settee. "Phin, you can set the bag here by this table. Stay with Celeste while we're with the doctor."

He shrugged and nodded, shoulders slouched.

Sam knocked on the connecting door.

A shadow moved behind the rippled, frosted glass, and the door opened. A young man about Sam's height wiped his hands on a cloth and smiled. "Hello, I'm Dr. O'Kelly. You just caught me. I was about to head for home. What can I do for you?" He noted Tick in Sam's arms and stepped back to allow them to enter. "You and your wife can both come in. How old is your son, and what seems to be his trouble?"

Surprise shot through Eldora, followed by red-hot embarrassment. Her tongue refused to say anything, and she stood there, feeling stupid.

Sam, easing Tick onto the examining table, jerked upright and spun around. "We're not married."

At the doctor's raised eyebrows, Eldora found her voice. "What he means to say is Tick isn't his son. He's not my son either. Tick's an orphan."

"Tick?"

"His given name is Michael, but everyone calls him Tick. I'm taking him from an orphanage in St. Louis to one in Denver, and Mr. Mackenzie has been kind enough to help."

"I see." The doctor peeled back the blankets, and Tick opened his eyes, giving a wispy smile. Then came what seemed hundreds of questions from the physician as he poked and prodded.

Some she could answer; some Tick supplied. Sam remained silent, arms crossed, leaning against a bookcase crammed with books and bottles and jars.

When Dr. O'Kelly listened to Tick's heart, first with his ear against the boy's chest and then with an instrument, his face grew grave.

The clock ticked on the wall and then chimed six times. Eldora's stomach rumbled, reminding her she'd been too anxious to eat anything at lunchtime.

The doctor ignored everything, closing his eyes. Furrows creased his forehead.

Tick's eyes rounded and locked onto Eldora's, and his narrow, bare chest rose and fell like a scared rabbit's. A faint bruise hovered over his breastbone where Phin had hit him that morning. His vulnerability made Eldora want to snatch him up and hold him tight.

Finally, the examination was over. Dr. O'Kelly patted Tick on the head and dug in a jar on his desk, producing a peppermint stick. "Here you go, young fellow. Why don't you climb down and go eat this in the waiting room? I'd like to talk to your"—he stopped and tilted his head toward Sam and Eldora—"to your friends here."

Tick nodded, his hair falling across his brow.

When the door closed behind him, the doctor stuffed the listening tool into his pocket and sat in the chair behind the desk. "Please, sit down."

Eldora's knees felt like putty, but she managed to get to a chair. O'Kelly's grave expression struck fear deep in her heart for the little boy.

"I won't beat around the bush. You've got a walking miracle there. I am surprised that he's gotten to the age of seven without treatment. Tick's got cardiac arrhythmia. Dizziness, weakness, tiredness, the fainting, they all point to it, and from what you say, his heart has stopped twice. That someone has been able to revive him with a heart punch even once is amazing."

"What is cardiac arrhythmia?" Eldora bit her bottom lip.

"In layman's terms, it's an irregular heartbeat. In Tick's case, his heart beats unusually fast, and from what I can tell, not effectively. His heart is beating so rapidly the blood hasn't time to be properly oxygenated before it is pushed through his system. He is often short of breath, and when he gets excited this is exacerbated."

Sam leaned forward with his forearms on his thighs. "What can we do for him?"

"He needs medication. I'm going to prescribe digitalis." He frowned. "The medicine should slow his heart rate and strengthen the heartbeats. Once he goes on the medication, he will need to stay on it. He's had this heart condition for as long as he can remember, so it isn't likely to just go away as he grows. Digitalis is what he needs."

She rolled the strange word around in her head. Though relieved there was some treatment to help Tick, her mind staggered. How would she afford the medication? Would the orphanage be willing to pay for it? And how would Tick ever be adopted? Who would take on a child who needed medication for the rest of his life?

"I've never given digitalis to so young a patient before, so I'd like to observe him for one night, possibly two, depending on the results. I can either watch him at your place of residence or admit him to the hospital."

Nodding, Sam said, "We're fresh off the train, Doc. Haven't even taken time to get rooms at a hotel. Maybe the hospital would be the best place." He looked at Eldora for her opinion.

Her throat closed, and her eyes burned. Hospitals were worse than orphanages. The thought of Tick lying in some high, white bed, all alone in a vast room of sick people, made her chest cave in. But what else could they do? She nodded.

Emerging from the examination room, her steps were wooden. Tick had broken the candy stick into three pieces. Her heart warmed at his generosity. Celeste hastened to jerk her scarf back over her face, but Eldora's quick glance at the doctor showed he had seen her deformity. Phin shoved the last bit of his candy into his mouth and crunched it, releasing a minty aroma into the air.

Sam put his big hand on Tick's shoulder. "Hey, kid. The doctor says he's got just what you need, some medicine to help your heart. Trick is he has to watch the dosage pretty close to get it just right, so he wants you to spend the night in the hospital so he can keep an eye on you. I told him you were a brave kid, and a night or two in the hospital wouldn't bother you a bit."

Even though Sam was talking to Tick, he was looking at Eldora, sending her the message that she needed to be brave, too. His strength and surety that they were doing the right thing strengthened Eldora's resolve. She squatted beside Tick and smiled. "Just think, when you have the right medicine you won't be keeling over. Phin won't have to sock you in the chest anymore."

Phin studied the doctor, shoving his hands in his pockets and staring under his hat brim. "Only a night or two?"

"That's right. I just want to keep an eye on him. You're Phin, right?" The doctor held out his hand. "It's a pleasure to meet you, young man. Your quick thinking saved Tick's life, and from what I hear, on more than one occasion. You're to be commended. Perhaps someday you'll be a physician yourself. You've got the instincts."

Phin shook the man's hand, his cheeks flushing. He toed the carpet and shrugged. Eldora hid a smile at his embarrassment. Few people praised Phin.

"Now, I'll take Tick with me. The hospital is just down the street here on Santa Fe. There's a hotel next door, good clean rooms and a restaurant." Dr. O'Kelly shrugged into his coat and put his hat on.

Eldora tried not to feel as if she were abandoning her responsibilities as they parted ways at the hospital door. The look Tick gave her over his shoulder formed a lump in her throat. She stuck her hand into her pocket and gripped the two silver dollars there, the only money she had.

&

Sam took Eldora's elbow and Celeste's hand and escorted them across the muddy side street to the hotel porch. Phin trotted beside him, the valise bumping his legs. For the tenth time that day Sam asked himself how he got saddled with a woman and three kids. And yet, he couldn't say he really minded. There was something about Eldora that intrigued him, brought out all his protectiveness. Those expressive eyes, her bird-delicate features, the way she handled the children, with affection but authority, too. So different from Yvette. Yvette took everything he gave her as her due, as his homage to her beauty. Eldora asked for nothing, was even surprised when he provided for her and the children. Her lack of acquisitiveness appealed to him.

And who could help falling for Celeste with her ravaged little face? The world had been unkind to her because of her deformity, but she retained a sweet nature that sought only to be invisible. Not to mention Tick, brave, weak as water, flying to the defense of anyone he thought needed help.

They reached the porch, and Phin thumped the valise down on the boards. The blanket from the train dangled over his shoulder, and he hitched it higher. He appraised the restaurant through the window before him, his eyes sparkling with a lean, hungry look. Sam appreciated his spunk. The boy was extremely loyal to those he considered his family.

They each had their challenges, but each had strengths, too. How did Korbin sleep at night knowing he'd all but cast them out on the street?

"Let's go." Sam set Celeste down and opened the door. Warmth and light and the smell of roasting meat greeted them. His mouth watered, and he sniffed the air. He passed the dining room door and stopped at the desk. With little trouble, Sam procured two rooms and had the bag sent up. He handed Eldora a key.

Lamplight played across her face, revealing her pale skin and the shadows under her eyes. She moistened her lips, and a little sigh escaped her. "I'm not sure the orphanage will reimburse you. We weren't supposed to be stopping at all. Mr. Korbin surely won't pay you back for the hotel." She took the key, but the worry lines on her face only deepened. "And there's the hospital and Tick's medicine. . ."

He wanted to comfort her somehow, to wipe the worry from her face. Though he could do nothing about her concern over Korbin's reaction, nor totally erase anxiety over Tick, at least he could ease her mind about her immediate future. "We'll talk about that later. Right now you need some food and some sleep, and so do the kids. Let's go on up. Phin and I can eat in the dining room, and I'll have a tray sent up for you and Celeste so you can eat in private, all right?" He winked at the little girl and cupped the back of her head to direct her to the stairs.

Her eyes crinkled above her scarf, rewarding him for remembering she didn't like to eat in public.

The hotel rooms were nothing to speak of, but at least they were clean. "Phin and I are next door. I'll have that food sent up as soon as I can."

She looked worn out, and who could blame her after the day they'd had? When he left, she was helping Celeste out of her shabby coat and yawning.

Sam and Phin entered the dining room and found a table near the front window. Consulting the menu, he ordered a tray sent up for the girls and the special of the day for himself and Phin.

Conversation flowed around them in the crowded room. China and glass clinked.

Phin's eyes never quit moving, taking in the patrons, the décor, the table service. He picked up his spoon and looked at his reflection in the back of it. "Steel. Guess you're used to silver, eh?"

Sam took a drink of water, noting the accusatory set of Phin's jaw. The boy was spoiling for a fight, as usual. "My family owns a silver mine. We do have silverware, but when I'm working up at the mine, I have a tin plate and a steel fork like everybody else."

A man at a nearby table dropped his wallet, and several coins rolled onto the carpet.

"Bet there are some good pickings in this lot." Phin took out his poker chip and walked it through his fingers, tilting his head at the customers. "I bet I could live for a couple months on the loose change alone."

"Who taught you to steal?" Sam leaned back as the waiter set a basket of bread on the table. Then he lifted it toward Phin to help himself first.

Phin's lips curved. "My Uncle Myatt. He said I was the best natural-born thief he'd ever seen. Didn't take me but a couple of days to master the seven bells. I was only six at the time."

"Seven bells?"

"Yep, Uncle Myatt tied seven little bells all over a coat and hung it on a tree. If I could get the wallet out of any of the pockets without ringing a single bell, then he knew I was ready to take to the train station or the fair or the market."

What kind of man taught his nephew to steal? Not only taught him but also boasted about the boy's ability? "You do know that stealing is wrong, even if you are good at it?" Sam tore open a roll and spread it with butter.

Phin scoffed. "So's beating orphans and giving them skimpy rations and not letting them see a doctor when they're sick. It's wrong to throw kids out just because their hearts don't work right or they were born with twisted lips. It was wrong for that rich lady to throw Eldora out on the street just because she wouldn't let the son of the house put his filthy paws on her. There's plenty of wrong in the world. I don't steal stuff to get rich. I steal to survive, to get food for the kids, or to make things easier for them." He crammed the bread into his mouth and reached for another. "You're sure," he spoke with his mouth full, "that Tick's gonna get fed in that hospital?" His eyebrows took a guilty tilt.

If Sam hadn't been watching closely, he never would've seen Phin slip a dinner roll into his pocket. "Tick's being fed, and so are the girls." He pursed his lips. "Go back to what you said about Eldora. She got thrown out?"

Phin shrugged. "Sure, more than once. The oldest orphans are farmed out to work wherever they can. Korbin placed her as a maid in three different houses, and every time something happened that got her sent back. The last place, one of the gents that lived there wanted to get fresh with her, and she slugged him for it." Phin shook his head. "There's those in this world that believe they can treat poor people any way they want to, and the poor people just have to take it, but that's wrong. Eldora has the right not to be bothered by the likes of him. Wish I'd have been there. I'd have done more than slap his face, I can tell you." His hands fisted on the edge of the table. "Eldora's tough, but she deserves to be protected." Phin directed his glittery black glare at Sam. "Don't you get any funny ideas about her either, or you'll have to deal with me."

Sam blinked, both amused and irritated at the boy's declaration. "I have no notion of getting embroiled with another female. I just slipped my neck out of that noose.

My motives in helping you all are pure. As a favor to my aunt, who is a new board member at the orphanage, I'm just looking out for you on the trip, that's all." And based upon the information he'd gathered from the kids so far, he had a long letter to write to Aunt Tabitha about what happened at the orphanage. She couldn't possibly be aware of the plight of the children, or she would do something about it and Mr. Korbin. "Eldora said she was almost twenty. Sometimes she doesn't seem much older than you."

"By rights she shouldn't have come back to the orphanage at all when she got fired, since she's too old now, but she didn't have any place else to go. I guess Korbin figured he'd get rid of her and us three all at the same time."

The waiter brought their food, and Phin ate as if it might be his last meal.

Sam toyed with his fork. How many times had the boy missed a meal or gone without so Tick and Celeste could have more? How often had he wondered where his next meal would come from?

"What did the doc say was wrong with Tick, and how long does he have to stay in the hospital?" Phin managed the questions between huge bites of potatoes and peas.

Sam, eating more slowly, explained what he understood about the diagnosis. "Doctor says he needs some medicine called digitalis, and that he'll need watching to make sure the dose is right. Might take a couple of days."

"Will the medicine cure him?"

"I don't know that there is a cure, but the medicine will help him out. It's something he's going to need for the rest of his life, I gather."

An arrow formed between Phin's black brows, and his chewing slowed. "Is it expensive?"

"I don't know. Some medicine can be very costly. I didn't

ask about the stuff Tick needs."

When Phin couldn't possibly eat another bite, Sam sent him upstairs. "I'm going to check on Tick, and I'll be back soon." He lowered his head to stare Phin right in the eye. "Don't get into any trouble while I'm gone."

The hospital windows were mostly dark when Sam arrived. Only a faint glow showed here and there. A nurse led Sam up the stairs to the ward.

Tick lay in a high cot, half in shadow with the lamp turned down low beside him. Rain pattered on the windows, and the strong smells of carbolic and vinegar hung in the air. Tick opened his eyes when Sam drew near.

"Hey there, Tick. How're you feeling? Did they feed you?" Sam eased onto the chair. Tick's bed was so high they were almost eye-to-eye. "No, don't try to sit up. Lie still."

"They fed me oatmeal." Tick made a face. His freckles stood out in his thin face like flecks of black pepper. But he had a little color to his cheeks, and his eyes were brighter. Perhaps the medicine was working already.

"You don't like oatmeal?"

He shook his head on the pillow. "You wouldn't either if you got it twice a day, every day."

"Twice a day?"

"Yep. Morning and noon. And salt-pork for supper." He stuck out his tongue. "The candy from the doctor was nice today. I like Dr. O'Kelly. But I don't like the medicine much. It doesn't taste so good."

"I don't imagine it does, but it appears to be helping you."

"It is." The doctor's voice surprised them both, and Sam turned in his chair. Dr. O'Kelly, wearing a white coat, stepped out of the shadows by the door. "I've come to check on you again, young man. Then you need to get to sleep."

Sam rose and backed up to give the doctor room.

After listening to the boy's heart for what seemed a very long time, the doctor straightened and smiled, rubbing Tick's head. "Better. Much better. Now, you snuggle down and sleep." He held the blanket up for Tick to wriggle farther under and tucked it in beneath his chin. "If you need anything, the nurse's desk is just outside the door."

"See you in the morning, Tick." Sam followed the doctor out the door and down to the first floor. "Doc, is he really better?"

"Yes, his heart rate has slowed, and his pulse is stronger. I'm going to increase the dosage in the morning by a few grains and see what effect that has. I'm very pleased with his reaction to the medicine so far. I'd like to see him get some meat on his bones though. Wherever you're headed, make sure he stays under a doctor's care. The dosage will have to be regulated as he grows and his activity levels change."

How likely was it that Tick would be under a doctor's care at an orphanage in Denver? The muscles in the back of Sam's neck tightened, but he nodded that he understood. "There's something else I wanted to ask you about." A nurse bustled by with an armload of linens. "In private."

Dr. O'Kelly's eyebrows rose, and he motioned for Sam to step into a side room. "This is one of the exam rooms. No one will bother us in here tonight." He took the chair from the corner and offered it to Sam, then leaned against the counter and crossed his arms. "What can I do for you?"

"It isn't about me. It's about the little girl who was with us today in your office."

O'Kelly nodded. "Remarkable blue eyes."

"She's real pretty and well-mannered, too. It's just such a shame about her lip. I was wondering if there wasn't something that could be done about it."

"She'd need a thorough examination to determine the extent of the deformity, but doctors have been operating on cleft lips for decades. Has she ever seen a surgeon about it?" He frowned and put his index finger along his upper lip. "No, I imagine she hasn't, not if she lived in the same orphanage as the little boy upstairs. Their neglect is criminal. Someone should report them to the proper authorities."

A spark of hope for Celeste burned in Sam's chest. How different would her life be without that gaping hole where her lip should be? "Don't you worry about that. I intend to see that the city of St. Louis knows what kind of treatment the orphans are receiving. Do you think you could take a look at Celeste in the morning? And how long would it take for the surgery and for her to recover?"

The doctor held up his hands. "Wait. I didn't say I could do the surgery. You need a surgeon who specializes in children's operations. I have a friend who would be just the man to treat Celeste. We went to medical school together. The trouble is he lives in Chicago now."

"Chicago, huh? Know anybody in Denver?"

"I can make inquiries. Bring the little girl to this room tomorrow morning at eight, and I'll take a look at her. Then I can write up some case notes to send with you." He frowned. "I was under the impression you were merely helping to get these children from one place to another. From your questions, it almost sounds as if you're considering taking on more than that."

It did sound that way. Sam studied his hands and pursed his lips, then shrugged. "I'm not committing to anything. I just wondered if there was anything you could do for the kid." He chuckled. "She hasn't said a single word to me. Quiet as can be. Just looks over that scarf at me with those big, blue eyes." He stood and started for the door.

The doctor followed him out into the hall toward the street entrance.

Sam held out his hand. "Thanks for everything you're doing, Doc. I'll see that the girl is here tomorrow morning for you to examine. Then, if you could give the case notes to Miss Carter, that would be fine. She's the one in charge of the kids. I'm just sort of helping her along a little. They're not really my concern."

The front door flung open, crashing into Sam's shoulder and sending him reeling backward into the wall. Dr. O'Kelly's eyes widened and he stepped back.

Eldora stood in the doorway, water streaming down her face and dripping off her clothes. She gasped, her chest heaving.

"What's wrong?" Sam asked.

She hadn't even taken the time to put on her shawl. Her dress clung to her, saturated with rain. "Sam, hurry. It's Phin." Her teeth chattered, whether from cold or from upset he couldn't tell.

"Is he hurt?" Sam slipped out of his coat and wrapped it around her shoulders, trying to ignore the pain screaming through his upper arm from the abrupt contact with the door.

She appeared not to notice when the heavy material closed around her, swallowing up her slight frame. Her icy hands gripped his, and she clung to him. "No, he's not hurt." She shook her head, sending droplets flying from the rats' tails of wet hair around her face. "At least I don't think so." Her teeth chattered.

"Then what?"

"He's been arrested."

eight

"I can't turn my back on you for two minutes. What were you thinking?" Eldora threw her hands up and paced the narrow space before the cell.

Phin sat on the edge of the wooden bunk, staring at the floor. His stony silence pushed Eldora closer to the brink of tears.

Weak morning sunlight, cold and clear after last night's rain, came through the window. She could see her breath and Phin's in the frosty air. The smells of damp wood, mud, and unwashed humanity assaulted her nose. How had Phin endured a night in this unheated cell with only a single, thin blanket for cover?

"This entire trip is like a raveled sweater. Every time I pull on a string, more comes undone." She blinked hard. "Tick in the hospital, Celeste's tantrum about seeing Dr. O'Kelly this morning—I had no idea such a well-behaved child could throw such a spectacular fit—and now you in jail for stealing." Hot tears pricked her eyes, but she quelled them. Tears were useless. Life just rolled right over her, in spite of tears.

Phin rose and crossed the narrow area between the bars and the far wall. "What did the sheriff say?"

"He said if I paid your fine he would release you."

"You are going to pay it, right?"

"With what? Air? The fine is ten whole dollars. I have exactly two. Two dollars to get four people to Denver. You tell me where I'm supposed to get ten dollars to pay a fine you never should've incurred in the first place."

"So what happens if you don't pay the fine? How long do I have to stay in here?"

She searched his countenance for a single shred of repentance or fear or even chagrin but read only defiance and stubbornness, and if she wasn't mistaken, a glint of pride.

"Sam's talking to the police officer now to find that out. Phin, why? And don't tell me it was for food. Sam said you ate enough for two grown men at supper, and the police found three dinner rolls stuffed in your pocket."

"I wasn't stealing food. Not that time."

"A wallet? A purse? You do know that stealing is wrong."

Phin stared at the wall behind her shoulder.

"Why, Phin? Why do you do it?"

"You're so smart, why don't you tell me?" He glared at her. "Always trying to boss me around, thinking you know what's going on in my head. You tell me why you think I steal stuff."

She'd had it with him. His stealing, his unreliability, his making her job harder at every turn. Leaving him here to learn a lesson appealed to her like it hadn't before. "I'll tell you why I think you steal. I think you're trying to get even with people for what your uncle did to you. I think you take your anger out on those around you, blaming them because you're an orphan."

"Don't talk about my uncle. He's going to come for me someday. I'm not an orphan like everyone else. I have family. And I don't plan to stay in Colorado. I only came along to get away from Korbin. If he thinks I'm in Denver, he won't be looking for me when I get back to St. Louis. I'll find somewhere in the city to hide and wait until my uncle comes back for me." He stopped pacing and tossed his hair off his forehead. A defiant gleam lit his eyes. "Then we'll be a family again."

Eldora prayed for patience and then promptly let fly. "Phineas Bartholomew, when are you going to get it through your thick head that your uncle isn't coming back? He dumped you in the orphanage to be rid of you the same way Celeste's family and Tick's family did. Too much time has passed for you to still cling to this stubborn hope that he's somehow going to waltz in and rescue you. The sooner you get over this notion, the better, because I'm sick of hearing it. You're an orphan like the rest of us, no better."

Red suffused his cheeks, and his fingers balled into fists. "You don't know what you're talking about." Tremors shook his rigid frame. "You're just jealous that I have family that's still alive and yours is dead. Uncle Myatt promised me he'd come back. He gave me his word."

"The word of a thief—someone who trains children to steal—isn't exactly gospel, you know. He lied to you so you wouldn't put up a fight when he left you, so you wouldn't try to follow him wherever he was going." She hated battering him this way, but someone had to make him see how things really were. His delusions were harming himself and those around him, and they had to stop. "Phin, I'm sorry, I really am. I wish your uncle had come back. I wish Tick's and Celeste's families had wanted them and loved them like they deserve. I wish I wasn't standing in a freezing jail worrying about all of you and trying to think of a way out of this mess. Mostly I wish you'd stop stealing and help me instead of making my job harder."

Inhaling sharply, his nostrils thinned, and he glared at her. "I was trying to help you."

"By breaking into a store? How would that help me?"

"I did it for Tick. Sam told me what kind of medicine he needed. I broke into the drugstore to get some."

Shock trickled through Eldora like little spiders. "But

Phin, the doctor was going to provide us with enough medicine to get to Denver. You didn't need to steal any."

"Just like a girl. You never think ahead. So we have enough to reach Denver. Then what? Sam says Tick will need the medicine for the rest of his life. Where do you think that's going to come from? The orphanage?" He spit out the word. "Nope, the minute we walk through those doors, Tick's medical treatment will quit. We'll be on our own again. Sam won't be there to pay for things and make people take care of us."

He wasn't saying anything Eldora hadn't feared, but hearing the words made the fear real. But what could she do? She could only cling to the truth she knew in her heart. "God will provide a way for us. He'll light the way for us, and His way won't involve breaking a commandment."

Phin snorted. "I can't see that God has bothered too much with us to this point. We're as alone now as we've ever been."

"You're wrong. He's with us. He brought Sam to us. Where would we have been without Sam? You got to ride in a private car, got served nice food off fine china, and Tick's being looked after properly at last. You would've had a nice warm bed last night, too, if you hadn't been so stupid."

"You're addle-brained if you think Sam is going to hang around after we get to Denver. For all the time you've spent telling me to quit holding onto a dream, you're spinning a few yourself. I see the way you look at him, like he was the president or a prince or something."

His words stung. She'd tried hard not to spin romantic notions about Sam, bracing herself for when he walked away, but he'd been so kind, it was hard. Shaking her head, she rallied. "I do nothing of the sort. Stop lashing out at me because you're mad. I told you a few truths you needed to hear. You need to get a grip on your temper and your bitterness before both land you in real trouble. You're in enough of a jam as it is. What Mr. Korbin will say, I don't know."

She rubbed her cold hands together. She had a fair idea. If Mr. Korbin were here right now, he'd say she was an incompetent fool and that Phin was getting exactly what he deserved.

"Who cares what that skunk would say? I'm better off in jail than anywhere near him. At least no one here has belted me." He sank onto the bunk and lay down, putting one knee up and throwing his arm over his eyes. "I still think you're an addle-headed girl."

"At least I'm not in jail."

Sam clenched and unclenched his hands, trying not to imagine them around that little scamp's throat. How could he upset Ellie like this? At least in jail Phin couldn't do anything else stupid to upset her.

Sam glanced at the door to the cells, wondering what she was saying to him. Probably coddling him, telling him everything would be all right, that she was sure he didn't mean to steal. Eldora Carter had a tender heart, and Phin took advantage of it at every turn.

Well, no more. The image of her soaking wet, cold right through, and desperately clinging to him out of fear for Phin rose in Sam's mind. The kid needed to learn that his misdeeds had consequences. She might coddle him, but that didn't mean Sam would.

"Ten dollars or ten days." The policeman crossed his arms and leaned back in his chair. "That's the standard fine for petty theft around here. Since he's a kid, and just passing through, we won't bother with a trial, not for something so small. He didn't even break a window to get in. Picked the lock as pretty as you please."

Sam didn't miss the admiration in the officer's voice, though he didn't share it. "I need to be on the train in three days if I'm going to make it home for Christmas. I could just pay the fine, but I'm not inclined to do that. What kind of lesson will he learn if I bail him out?"

The lawman pursed his lips and rubbed his moustache. "Christmas. That's rough." He leaned forward and shuffled the papers on his desk. "Tell you what. He can work it off. If he works today and tomorrow for the city, I'll release him to get on the train Sunday morning. Can't do better than that."

They shook hands on the deal, and Sam followed the officer into the next room.

"Well?" Phin bounded up, grabbed the bars, and thrust his thin face forward. "When can I get out of here? Did you pay the fine?"

Sam studied Eldora. Her cheeks were flushed, but she didn't look like she'd been crying. Her delicate throat worked and she exhaled, her breath showing in a puff of crystals. That thin shawl couldn't be keeping her very warm, and he was conscious of the weight and warmth of his own heavy coat. His jaw set. "No."

She turned those big eyes on him, and he felt like a worm. Her eyebrows arched, and she blinked. "No?" Her lips remained parted.

Sam shoved his hands in his pockets. "The officer and I feel it would be best for Phin to work off his fine."

It was Phin's turn to gape. "Work it off? How?"

Keys jangling, the policeman stepped forward. "You'll be sweeping sidewalks, cleaning the streets, and emptying the spittoons in the public buildings." He inserted one of the keys and cranked it over, opening the door. Withdrawing a pair of shackles from his belt, he slipped one on Phin's thin wrist and let out a piercing whistle.

Eldora jumped a foot, and Sam put his hand on her arm to steady her.

A burly constable shouldered his way into the cell area. "You want something, boss?"

"I do. Take this young man out to do some service for the community. Start with the courthouse. He can sweep the floors and empty the spittoons."

"Sir," Eldora asked, "are the shackles necessary?"

"They are. If he's out of the cell and not actually working, he'll be cuffed to the constable here." With a snap, the cuff closed around the young officer's wrist.

Phin scowled at Sam. "This is the best you could do? I thought you'd pay the fine."

"You thought wrong. You know, you're a rotten thief. I've only known you a few days, and you've been caught stealing three times."

Phin's mutinous glare turned into a smirk as the constable headed him out the door. "You don't know how many times I *don't* get caught."

Sam didn't know whether to laugh or yell, so he gritted his teeth. Phin was the epitome of unrepentant arrogance. A little time cleaning spittoons and sweeping up the dung on the streets would do him a world of good. In the meantime, Sam didn't intend to go another hour without taking care of another problem that needed tending to.

"Let's go check on Tick. The nurse said Celeste could sit with Tick for a while, but I'm sure she's getting restless." He put his hand under Eldora's elbow and steered her out. "I never would've suspected Celeste could be so. . ."

"Strong-willed?"

"Yes. I never thought she'd break down like that. Poor kid. How did you convince her finally to let the doctor at least look at her lip?"

"I had to promise to hold her hand through everything, and I had to promise that he wouldn't laugh or make fun of her or hurt her in any way. Dr. O'Kelly was so kind and matter of fact. He didn't recoil or even talk about her lip the whole time he examined her. He talked about his new puppy. It seems he got a new spaniel pup a couple of weeks ago, and he told her all about the dog's antics and made up a few adventures about him, too. In the end, she forgot to be afraid or self-conscious, though she refused to answer any of his questions. He promised to bring the puppy to the hospital for her and Tick to see this afternoon."

They crossed the street and walked up the two blocks to the hospital. The wind whipped her skirts and tugged her hair from its braid. She clutched her shawl under her chin and leaned into the breeze. He held her elbow with one hand and anchored his hat with the other. When they reached the calm of the hospital foyer, she blew on her hands and shivered, then tried to tuck wisps of wayward hair behind her ears.

"Run up and get Celeste, and then we have an errand or two to see to." He waited at the bottom of the stairs, eager to get going now that he'd made up his mind what he wanted to do.

When the girls reached the bottom of the stairs, he took Celeste's hand and Eldora's elbow and led them back out into the wind. Good thing the Emporium was only in the next block.

The bell overhead jangled when he opened it, and they stepped inside.

Celeste gave a gasp, and her blue eyes widened. Eldora wasn't much different, trying to see everything in the packed store at once. The little girl dropped his hand and took Eldora's, pointing to a glass case full of jars of candy.

Eldora seemed to remember her manners and turned to him. "Was there something you needed to pick up?"

"I need quite a few things, actually. Hopefully you can help me."

"Of course." She let her fingers drift across the polished wood on the edge of the counter. "I don't have much experience shopping, but anything I can do to help I will."

"I haven't the slightest doubt that you'll be more than up to the task." He nodded to the sales clerk headed their way.

"How can I help you?" The woman tucked a pencil behind her ear and brushed the front of her white apron. "My, what a pretty young'un you have." She tilted her head to one side. "I'm trying to decide who she favors. Must be you, sir, with the blue eyes."

Sam didn't bother to correct her, giving the girls a wink when the clerk turned her back to straighten some boxes on the shelf behind her. "You seem to have a nice selection of ready-made clothing available. I'm looking for new clothes."

Eldora's eyebrows rose and bunched, but she still didn't ask her questions aloud. The saleswoman nodded and pulled a tablet toward her. "What size?" She flicked a glance at him, appraising his build.

"Several sizes. The clothing isn't for me. It's for Miss Carter and Celeste here. Also for two boys, one about seven and one around thirteen." Sam held his hand level with his waist and then raised it to mid-chest. "About so high for each of them."

"Sam," Eldora breathed, "you don't—"

"Don't argue." He took her hand and tugged her away a few steps. "Celeste, you stay right there." When they were at the far end of the store, standing among the garden tools and hardware, he stared straight into her eyes. "You all need new clothes, warmer clothes. I feel like a cad in my heavy coat when you're getting by with nothing but a shawl." He gestured to the frayed edge.

Pink flooded her cheeks, and her lips flattened. "I'm sorry if we shame you."

Guilt stabbed him. He'd said the wrong thing. "No, no. I'm not in the least ashamed of you." He squeezed her chilly hands. "You've done more with less better than any person I've ever met. It's just that I have so much, and you have so little. Please, let me do this for you and the kids. It won't do Tick much good to come out of the hospital and get a chill because his coat is too small and worn out to keep him warm. And Celeste's wrists stick out of her dress. They'll be better off with clothes and shoes that fit and function." He tilted his head to the side and entreated her.

"You know the orphanage won't authorize the expense. They won't reimburse you."

"I'm not worried about that."

She stared at their joined hands for a long time without speaking.

"Is it such a difficult decision?"

"If it was only for myself I would refuse, but you are right. The children need warmer clothes."

"So do you."

"No." She shook her head. "The children's needs are one thing. I can't let you buy anything for me. It wouldn't be proper." She bit on her lower lip. "I wouldn't feel right knowing I could never repay you."

He released her hands and shook his head. Rubbing his palm on the back of his neck, he contemplated her. Yvette had taken with both hands, though she had no real need of the baubles and fripperies he'd bought for her, and here stood Ellie in threadbare clothing and worn-out boots, refusing necessities for fear of owing a debt she couldn't pay.

"I tell you what. You can consider it an early Christmas gift. It's rude to refuse a gift, and if you don't pick out the stuff yourself, I'll have to do it. Now, stop arguing with me and start shopping." He stepped aside for her to walk up the packed aisle, hoping she'd acquiesce to his authority.

Another thought occurred to him, something Phin had shared at dinner the night before. He reached for her hand once more. "I assure you I'm not looking to be repaid for anything, not with money and not any other way." He waited until understanding dawned in her brown eyes.

Again pink raced up her cheeks, and she nodded.

nine

Though she was grateful to be getting back on the train and continuing their journey after so many days in Salina, Eldora couldn't help but feel it was wrong to be traveling on a Sunday morning. The rain from the past few days had turned to sleet in the night, coating every surface with a layer of glittering ice. Her brand-new shoes slid on the frozen ruts of the rail yard, and she lurched.

Sam's strong hand came under her elbow and steadied her. "Whoops. A little slippery." He winked at Tick, high on his other arm. "At least the sun is finally shining."

The Mackenzie railcar, its dark-green paint and brass rails gleaming, stood just ahead, the last in the train. Frosty crystals hung in the air, shreds of the clouds of steam emanating from the hulking engine far to their right up the line ahead of the passenger, freight, and mail cars.

Entering Sam's private car felt familiar and yet strange. Like her new clothes. She squeezed her shoulders together inside her new wool coat, luxuriating in the warmth and heaviness but uneasy at taking so much from him.

Phin shucked his coat to reveal a smart new tweed jacket and pants. He'd been even more reluctant than Eldora to take anything from Sam, but in the end, Sam had his way. Though Phin pretended not to be impressed with the new outfit, Eldora caught him fingering the edge of his jacket or the sturdy buttons on his shirtfront several times.

A porter carried their bags, the old, beat-up valise and a shiny, new leather case, to their rooms.

Sam waited for a second porter to bring his bags befor letting Tick slide down until he landed on the settee. "Don take your coat off yet. Let it warm up in here a bit. Once th engine gets going, the radiators will heat up." He ducke outside to speak to the conductor, a different man from th martinet on the last train.

Celeste sat beside Tick, her feet together in her gloss black boots. She stroked the edges of her cape, seemingl unable to stop touching the soft fur. Her black hood frame her face, and the blue scarf Sam had chosen for her made he eyes even more brilliant.

Tick bounced on his seat, his cheeks pink from the col and better health. He knelt on the upholstery and peered ou the window at Sam. "Eldora, he's pretty swell, isn't he? Ne clothes for us, and food and medicine and candy." He flashe a grin over his shoulder, a faint ring of stickiness testament t the peppermints he'd consumed that morning.

Sam *was* pretty swell, to use Tick's description, but Eldor knew she must steel her heart against him. A headach pinged behind her eyes, reminding her of her sleepless nigh tossing and turning, worrying about the children, bein squashed under the responsibility she bore and tortured wit thoughts of Sam and the mounting debts she owed him.

She heard once again the cautions of a kindly woman wh had come to teach a Sunday school for the orphan girls once *"You are so vulnerable, more than most. Without fathers an brothers to look after you, you're easy prey for men once you leav here. If you aren't taken advantage of, then you're in danger o giving your heart too easily to the wrong man. Starved for lov and affection as you are, any kindness or flattery might turn you head. I know from experience, for I was once a girl newly turne out of an orphanage. I married the first man who came along and I have lived to regret it. So, beware, all of you. Don't spir*

*reams about romance and rescue. You'll wind up hurt and more
lone than ever before."*

Though Eldora hadn't understood at the time everything
the woman was trying to caution them against, she had come
o realize the truth and wisdom in the warning. Too many
f her fellow orphan girls, once released into the world, had
ecome street walkers or virtual slaves in the workhouses,
r had married men who abused and mistreated them.
ven those like Eldora who had found work as domestics
ere considered easy pickings for the male members of the
ouseholds, as she had encountered firsthand.

But was Sam like that? He claimed to want nothing in
eturn for his kindness. In every way, he had behaved as a
entleman should. But why? What did he have to gain?
What did he want from them, *from her,* in exchange?

She couldn't deny that every time she was near him her
reath came a little faster and her heart began to trip and
tall. The way he had with the children, even the prickly
hin, made her middle feel mushy and warm, and sometimes
vhen he looked right at her she forgot to breathe altogether.

*Stop it, Eldora. You're in danger of making a complete fool of
ourself. A man like Sam Mackenzie would never be interested in
n ugly duckling like you, poorer than a muskrat, with no proper
chooling. If you let yourself dream romantic notions about him,
ou're just going to get your heart broken when he leaves you in
Denver. Get through the next two days with your wits and your
eart intact.*

Something tugged her sleeve. She looked down into Tick's
ace.

"I said, 'He's pretty swell, isn't he?'"

She smoothed his fair hair out of his eyes and nodded, a
ump in her throat. "Yes, he's pretty swell, but Tick. . ." She
vanted to caution him against hero worship, against giving

his little heart to someone who would walk away from ther
but somehow she couldn't do it, couldn't rub the bloom o
his obvious admiration for Sam. He'd know heartache soc
enough without her hurrying it along.

The train shuddered, and Sam swung up onto the platfor
and entered the car. He braced his legs as the train jerke
and then slid into motion. "Two days to Denver." He too
the seat beside Eldora. The smells of coal smoke, cold a
and shaving soap clung to him.

She slid down the settee and fussed with helping Celes
remove her cloak and hood.

"Kids, there's some hot cocoa and cookies down in th
dining room." Sam pointed to the rear of the car. "You hea
on back there. I want to talk to Eldora for a minute, and the
we'll join you."

Eldora's palms prickled, and her throat went dry. She ha
to get over this silly-girl attraction to him. Securing a polit
expression on her face that she prayed gave nothing away, sh
waited.

Tick and Celeste went without having to be asked twic
but Phin remained, his hands in his pockets. The suspiciou
tilt of his eyebrows and the set of his jaw both touched an
exasperated Eldora. "Go ahead, Phin. We'll be right along."

Sam tugged off his gloves and stuffed them in his pocke
"He can't quite bring himself to trust me, can he?"

With her hands folded in her lap, she shrugged. "H
doesn't really trust anyone. You'll notice he's not speakin
to me. I'm afraid we had some harsh words when he wa
in jail, words he needed to hear but that I spoke in anger
Heaviness dragged at her. "What was it you wanted to spea
to me about?"

"Quite a few things, actually. We hardly ever seem to b
alone, what with one crisis with the children or another. No

guess I know how a parent feels." He chuckled, and a spark of longing flared in Eldora. "I wanted to tell you what the doctor said about Celeste." He dug in his inner coat pocket and pulled out some folded papers. "He wrote some notes up for you to give to the doctor in Denver, both for her and for Tick." The pages crackled as he smoothed them out. "He seems to think she's an excellent candidate for surgery to correct her problem. Said she'd have a small scar where that gaping hole is now, and she'd be able to eat normally, breathe better, talk clearer, and would probably have fewer problems with her ears and with catching colds."

Hope clashed with reality in her breast. She took the papers, not seeing the words. He just didn't get it. In his own way, he was in as great a need to hear and resign himself to the truth about these kids' futures as Phin had been about his uncle. "Sam, you've been very good to us, and I thank you for all you've done, but you need to understand something. Celeste won't be getting surgery. Tick most likely won't have another dose of medicine once the supply the doctor gave us runs out. When we get to Denver, we won't be going to nice homes. We'll be going to an orphanage. Probably one that has all it can do just to keep kids fed and clothed. There's no extra money for medicines and surgeries. Without adoption, their future is hardly secure, and who will adopt any of them?"

She couldn't sit still any longer. The fears and knowledge she had wrestled with all night spilled out, and she had to move away from him. The train swayed, but she caught the rhythm and paced to its roll. "Who would adopt Celeste, with her face like that and knowing an expensive surgery is needed? If she got adopted, it would most likely be by someone who only wanted to abuse her or work her to death. Once she is too old for the orphanage, she'll be turned out, and how can she hope to get a decent job? Then there's Tick. No one will want him, knowing of his heart trouble and that a lifetime of drug expenses lies ahead. If he lives to be an adult—and what are his chances without the medicine—what kind of work can he do? Nothing physical, and his education thus far is pathetic." She swung her hands, trying to make him see her point. "Not to mention Phin. He's destined for prison, the way he's going. Who would adopt him, knowing they'd have to nail down everything in the place to keep him from stealing it? I'm responsible for them, and I can't do a thing to help them." Panic welled in her chest and choked off her airway. She tried to close her eyes and ward it off, but that disrupted her balance. Lurching against a table, she pushed aside his steadying hand. "What's going to happen to them?"

Sam grabbed her arms and tugged her against him. His large hand came up to cup the back of her head, and she realized she was on the verge of sobbing. "Shhh, Ellie, I'm sorry. I didn't mean to upset you. I understand you're scared, but everything will be all right."

His kind words coupled with the strong, protective feel of his arms around her broke through the tissue-thin walls she'd tried erecting around her heart. Swaying with the movement of the train, she tilted her head back to look into his eyes, but her gaze got caught on his lips. Finely molded, gently curving. . .

The instant she knew she wanted him to kiss her, she jolted backward out of his grasp. "What can a rich man like you know of our troubles? You snap your fingers, and whatever you desire comes to pass. Your life is light and freedom. Ours is darkness and no choices." Words sprang out of her mouth, stupid words hurled at him to try to dodge the guilt and fear stabbing her. "The children adore you, even Phin, though he's trying hard not to show it, but what happens to them when you leave us—I mean. . .them? Where will they be then?"

Where will I be when you leave me? Her insides turned to a quivering mass as the reality of her feelings hit her.

"Ellie, please—"

"Don't call me Ellie!" Pain cleaved her heart, knowing she had been foolish enough to fall in love with him and knowing there was no hope along that path. To her mortification, the tears slipped over her lashes, and a strangled sob exploded from her throat. She fled into her sleeping compartment, slammed the door, and threw herself across the bed.

❧

Sam's shoulders slumped, and he sank into a chair, as battered as if he'd fallen down a mineshaft. Here he'd meant only to encourage her with his good news about Celeste, and she'd detonated like a pint of nitro. The memory of her tears lashed him like a whip.

At least they were real tears, real emotion spawned by real problems. Her choking cries, muffled through the wall behind him, made him close his eyes and fist his hands, leaning his head on the paneling.

Yvette had cried prettily, dabbing at her lashes with a lace handkerchief, darting sidelong looks at him to gauge his reaction and coming out of her sorrow the instant she got what she wanted. Manipulative minx, and he, like a first-class chump, had fallen for it for a time. A scowl twisted his mouth. Why was he thinking of Yvette now?

After a few minutes, the crying sounds ceased, or at least grew so faint he couldn't make them out. He rose and edged down the narrow passageway to listen at her door. Should he tap? Perhaps she was asleep. The shadows under her eyes this morning made him wonder if she'd slept at all last night, and who could blame her? She'd certainly been under a lot of strain, and the glimpse she had given him into the children's futures would have kept him awake under the circumstances. He decided not to disturb her, knowing he wouldn't have any idea what to say to her if she answered the door. He'd best check on the kids.

Tick and Celeste sat at the table, Phin leaned against the wall, and none of them were eating the cookies. Phin's glare could've set Sam's suit on fire.

"What?" Still tender from the scene with Ellie—Eldora— he was in no mood to deal with anything from Phin.

"We heard you. We all came to get you, because Tick didn't want to start in on the cookies without you and Eldora."

Tick's lower lip jutted. "You made her cry."

Fear that they might've heard the discussion of their futures clawed up his chest. "What else did you hear?"

Celeste had tucked her scarf up again and leveled an unnaturally mature stare at him. Phin shoved away from the wall and flung himself into a chair. "Nothing we didn't already know, and nothing you shouldn't have figured out. Why do you think we're on this train? Because nobody will adopt us in the whole city of St. Louis, and Korbin wanted to get rid of us. He's making us someone else's problem."

Their resigned acceptance of their lot in life tore at Sam. His own childhood, so secure in the love and care of his parents, mocked him. Ellie—Eldora—was right. He knew nothing of the suffering they'd endured, the uncertainty, the lack of affection and security. He had thought getting them to Denver would be enough, that he'd leave them at the orphanage, fulfilling his promise to Aunt Tabitha and doing his good deed. But the notion of leaving them there— especially knowing how precarious their futures would be there—didn't sit right with him. But what could he do?

"Why doesn't she like to be called Ellie?" The question was out before he realized it.

Phin rolled his eyes. "She told us she used to be Ellie—that's what her dad called her—but when she came to the orphanage, the matron called her by her full name, Eldora. She says Ellie is for the happier times, when she had a family. Eldora is her orphan name."

"Like Tick's mine." The little boy nodded as if this made complete sense. "I ain't been called Michael in a long time, but if I was ever gonna get a family someday, I'd let them call me Michael. I don't guess Eldora will want to be called Ellie until she has a family again."

"Does everyone have two names?"

Phin shook his head. "Nope, not when they're foundlings. The women in the orphanage nursery name the kids who show up as babies. She"—he jerked his thumb at Celeste—"got dumped on the orphanage doorstep on a clear night with lots of stars, so they named her Celeste. One of the schoolteachers we had for a while, Mr. Plimpkin, told her it meant 'from the heavens' or 'from the stars' or something silly like that."

Sam raised a smile for the little girl. "I don't think that's silly at all. It's a beautiful name, and she wears it well." He fingered the edge of the tablecloth where it fell against his leg. So, Ellie was for the happy times. He fervently hoped someday she'd get to use the name again. She deserved to be happy.

"I'm going to find the conductor and see about getting some food ordered in for lunch. You kids stay here, and don't disturb Eldora. She'll come out when she's ready." He rose. "Phin—"

"I know, don't leave the car."

As he headed up the passageway, Tick's piping little voice reached him. "Phin, is what Eldora said true? Will Sam leave us when we get to Denver?"

Sam froze.

"Of course he will, you twit. He's just looking after us as a favor to that dried-up old aunt of his that we saw at the station in St. Louis. What did you think? That he was going to adopt you or something? You're worse than a girl for pipe dreams. He'll drop us like a hot rock as soon as he can."

Stung and not wanting to hear whatever other aspersions Phin might cast on his character, Sam stalked away. How had Phin struck so close to the truth?

ten

"I sent a telegram from the last stop so transport will be waiting when we arrive." Sam slid his watch out of his pocket. "We should be pulling into the station soon."

Eldora nodded. Her skin stretched taut over her cheekbones, and the dark smudges hadn't left the hollows under her eyes.

Several times over the past two days he'd tried to engage her in conversation, but she remained aloof. Though he knew he'd hurt her, he didn't have a clue as to what he had done that was so terrible. Provided them with food, safe and comfortable travel, medical care, kindness. He clenched his back teeth.

Phin and Tick's accusatory glares didn't help the situation either. At least Celeste wasn't shooting daggers his way with every glance. No, she just avoided looking at him altogether.

"If it weren't dark, you could see the mountains by now."

No one responded.

Eldora dug in her handbag and produced the box from the drugstore. She lifted one of the twists of paper out and emptied the contents into a cup of water. "Here, Tick, time for your medicine."

The youngster made a face but gulped the stuff down, swiping his mouth with the back of his hand and giving the cup back to Eldora. "Thanks."

Tick, one good change. Each day he seemed stronger, had more color in his cheeks, and he certainly had an appetite. The child could eat more than Sam and Phin combined, it seemed.

With almost imperceptible slowness, the train decelerated as they neared the Denver depot. Hundreds of train cars slid by the windows—boxcars, ore cars, and passenger cars. Lights and buildings. "We'll have to cross over several tracks to get to the depot, so everyone keep hold of a hand." The last thing he wanted was to lose someone in the dark rail yard or in the busy depot. "We'll climb a flight of stairs to get to street level. That's where Buckford will meet us with the sleigh."

They rose as one and lined up by the door. Prisoners going to the dock. Why did he feel like an executioner? His promise to his aunt was almost fulfilled. Soon he'd be having supper with David and Karen, and tomorrow he'd be on the train to Martin City, home in time for Christmas.

The snow was a foot deep in places, so he picked Tick up. Two porters and Phin carried the bags, and they wove their way along with the other passengers to the brightly lit platform.

The instant their feet hit the boards, Tick wriggled to get down. He marched over to Eldora and took her hand, staring hard at Sam to be sure everyone knew where his allegiance lay.

"This way." Their footsteps crunched on the damp concrete stairs leading to the street. Voices echoed off the tiled walls and were swallowed up when they reached the high-ceilinged waiting room. The smell of damp wool and wood smoke, people and cold weather, wrapped around him. Ushering his little group to a backwater corner where they wouldn't be jostled, he scanned the crowd for a familiar face.

"Lookit that." Tick pointed. Every window and wall was festooned with garlands and ribbon. Red and silver ornaments glinted in the gaslight. In the far corner, near the huge fireplace, a quartet broke into a Christmas carol. Each time the doors opened, a gust of wind brought in the tinkling sound of sleigh bells.

"Wonder what Christmas is like at this orphanage. In St. Louis, we got to eat ham, and every kid got new socks or gloves or something." Phin kicked his heel against the wall, his hands shoved deep in his pockets.

Eldora's eyes were huge. "I'm sure it will be nice. Maybe there will be some decorations, or even some toys." She didn't sound as if she believed what she was saying. And what kind of Christmas was it for a kid without toys?

The crowd parted a little, and he spied Buckford waiting by the door. Swinging his arm overhead, Sam flagged the friend and family butler.

Impeccably dressed in a wool topcoat and bowler, Buckford clasped Sam's offered hand. "Hello, sir. Good to see you back again."

"Hello, Buckford. Glad you got my message. You brought the big sleigh?"

"Yes, sir."

"Good. Buckford, this is Eldora Carter, and these are her charges: Phin, Celeste, and Tick. We're driving them out to the orphanage."

"Very good, sir." Not so much as a lift of the eyebrow or a twitch of the lip. For as long as Sam had known Buckford—and that was most of his adult life—he had been unable to crack the butler's shell of decorum. He looked each one over, a polite smile on his seemingly ageless face, and bowed to Eldora. "I'm pleased to meet you. It's quite an endeavor, traveling across the country with children. I hope you had a pleasant journey."

Eldora blinked and nodded. "Thank you. It was fine. Mr. Mackenzie was most helpful."

"His mother will be pleased to hear it." A twinkle lit Buckford's eye, and he turned to the children.

Phin stuck out his hand—Sam watched closely, knowing Phin's proclivities—and shook Buckford's. Tick copied the older boy, pretending bravado, but his cheeks were pale.

When Buckford's gaze landed on Celeste, he stopped, took a second look at her pretty eyes and roses-and-cream complexion, and bowed deeply. "Miss Celeste, it is my pleasure."

The sound that came from the little girl could only be described as a giggle, the first Sam had heard her utter. Hmm. He blinked. How had Buckford managed that?

The butler chucked her under the chin and patted her head. And, of all things, when he held out his hand, Celeste took it, her nose wrinkling in a grin above her scarf.

Eldora seemed taken aback by this instant rapport as well, staring from one to the other, her lips parted.

Buckford led the way outside to the waiting sleigh, holding the little girl's hand and leaving Phin and Sam to wrestle the luggage.

Sam piled kids and bags in and tucked buffalo robes around them. He handed Eldora in as if she were spun glass and received a whispered thank you, then vaulted himself up onto the front seat to ride beside Buckford. With a clash of bells, the horses took off.

They traveled several blocks before Sam couldn't stand it anymore. "Aren't you going to ask me about them?" He ducked his head deeper into his collar to shield him from the wind their quick passage created.

"Do you want to tell me, sir?"

"I'm watching out for them as a favor to Aunt Tabitha." Buckford had worked for Tabitha Mackenzie before coming to Sam's parents' employ. Now he worked for Sam's brother and his wife, mostly at their townhouse here in Denver. "I'm supposed to see they get to the orphanage here without trouble."

"And have you had trouble? Your brother expected you several days ago. They've delayed traveling to Martin City, waiting for your arrival."

"He got my message, didn't he? About stopping over in Salina?"

"Yes."

"How's Karen feeling?"

"Doing well. Anxious for Christmas. She's looking forward to seeing your parents again. As am I." Buckford steered the horses around a corner and headed toward the south end of the city. "David hovers and fusses, and she pretends to like it. They're both very excited about the little one."

"Almost as excited as my parents, I bet. The first grand-child." Sam grinned. "I bet Dad is hardly fit to live with."

"Mr. Mackenzie even sent me a cigar, though neither of us smokes."

"That sounds like him."

They rode in silence, and Sam checked over his shoulder every few blocks. The kids were all eyes, watching the houses and buildings flash by. Eldora seemed not to see any of it. She kept her eyes straight ahead and appeared lost in thought—or worry if the crease between her eyebrows was any indication.

The buildings and houses grew farther apart as they left the city center, and eventually the only thing on the horizon was a black, square-shaped edifice alone out on the east face of a foothill. "Is that the place?"

"Yes." Buckford slapped the lines.

"Why is it so far out of town?"

"Cheap land, most likely. That and there's room to expand."

"More like they want to keep the whole thing out of sight."

The closer they got, the uglier the building grew. In a complete revolt against graceful architecture, the solid stone

walls and blank rectangular windows looked more like those
of a prison than a home for children. Cold seeped into Sam's
bones that had nothing to do with the outside temperature.
Well, maybe it was more cheerful on the inside. At least
those thick walls would keep the wind out.

Buckford pulled the sleigh onto the horseshoe drive,
passing between the gateposts and beneath the iron sign
declaring this indeed to be the Denver Orphanage.

Since when did doing exactly what he was supposed to do
fill Sam with such dread?

❧

Eldora's throat closed, and her hands ached from clenching
them beneath the heavy buffalo robe. The orphanage looked
much worse than it had in her mind. Cold, imposing,
unfriendly. Home to the children now and home for her
if she could get them to hire her on. She'd decided, after
sobbing her heart out on the train, that she couldn't leave the
children here alone and go back to St. Louis as if she didn't
care. Mr. Korbin would be as relieved to be rid of her as he
was the children. She could clean or do laundry or sew or
even care for the babies in the nursery. Surely somewhere in
this hulking building they could find room for her.

The sleigh pulled to a stop with a final clash of bells.
Eldora clambered down without waiting for Sam's help,
determined to take charge of the situation and stand on
her own two feet. The past two days, being with him in the
close confines of the railcar and knowing their time together
was getting small, had been torture. She knew she had been
distant and unkind, but it was the only way she knew to deal
with the pain. His puzzled glances and halting efforts to
draw her out of her shell only made her retreat faster.

Weights pulled at her legs with every step across the snow-
packed drive. They mounted the stairs, Celeste clinging

to Buckford's hand in a thoroughly uncharacteristic way and Phin and Tick dragging their feet. Sam held the door. Once in the foyer, the children lined up along the wall in a formation all too familiar to Eldora for having performed it so often herself. Their faces lost all the animation and life they had displayed on the journey.

From the end of the long hallway, the sounds of cutlery and plates clattered. The smell of cooked cabbage, as familiar to her as the lining up of children, assaulted her nose. Dinner in full swing.

She tugged off her gloves and smoothed her hair as best she could. At least, thanks to Sam's generosity, they all looked respectable in new clothes. "You children wait right here. I'm going to see the matron or the superintendent or whoever is about at this hour. Phin, keep an eye on the younger kids and don't stray."

Bracing herself, she turned to Sam and held out her hand. "Thank you for all your help in getting us here. We are most appreciative. I don't know what I would've done without your assistance." She kept her tone and her words as formal as possible, in spite of the overwhelming feeling of despair and abandonment that threatened to swamp her. "I'm sure you want to be on your way to your relatives' house, so we won't keep you."

Sam shoved his hat back, a puzzled expression on his face. "If it's all the same to you, I'll talk to the superintendent. I'd like to satisfy myself that the kids will be taken care of." He reached out his long arm past her and rapped on the office door.

On the staircase above them, someone cleared her throat. "Excuse me? May I help you?"

Eldora stepped out so she could see better. A thin-faced woman with pale yellow hair shot through with gray leaned over the banister. The light from the lamp she carried cast a golden glow over her features.

"I'm looking for the superintendent or the matron." Eldora unbuttoned her coat to get at the papers Mr. Korbin had sent.

"Mr. Korbin and Mrs. Phillips are at dinner."

"Mr. Korbin?" Eldora stopped.

The woman came down the stairs. "Yes, Mr. Finlo Korbin. He's the super here."

Sam stepped closer and whispered to Eldora, "Maybe he's a relative?" Then he turned to the woman, smiling and charming. "Miss, would you please tell the superintendent we want to see him? These kids have come a long way, and they're tired and hungry."

"Of course. I'm Miss Templeton." Her smile changed her face from plain to pretty in an instant, responding to Sam's friendliness. She set the lamp on the hall table and hurried away, eager to do his bidding.

Eldora clamped her lips shut. So much for taking charge and freeing Sam from his self-assumed responsibilities.

A lean man in a dark suit strode down the hallway, dabbing his lips with a napkin. One glance told her he must be related to Conrad Korbin.

"You wanted to see me? I'm Finlo Korbin, superintendent of this orphanage." He ignored Eldora and offered his hand to Sam. "What can I do for you?"

"Can we step into your office?"

"Of course." The super studied each of the lined-up children for a few seconds and then turned and opened the office door. "Miss Templeton, light the lamps."

Wanting to exert the little authority she had, to show her competence before the super so that he might look favorably on hiring her, Eldora put her hand on Sam's arm. "I will take care of things. You don't need to stay."

"Don't be ridiculous."

"Please, Sam. I need to do this myself. At least wait here with the children while I speak to Mr. Korbin."

With a frown, he backed up and let her enter the office alone.

Miss Templeton put matches to lamps and brought a very utilitarian room to light. Immense desk, straight-backed chairs, rank of filing cabinets. No pictures, no adornments of any kind. Eldora gathered her courage, stepped forward, and laid out the paperwork on his desk. "My name is Miss Carter, and I've come from the St. Louis Children's Home. Mr. Conrad Korbin sends his greetings."

"My brother?" He reached for the papers and unfolded them.

So that was the relation. Eldora laced her fingers at her waist and waited for him to finish reading the letter explaining the arrival of the children and her.

Finlo tipped the pages toward the light, and as he read, his face hardened. Slowly, he lowered the pages. "Is this some kind of joke?"

A sinking feeling trickled through her. "No, sir." She swallowed.

"Impossible. There is no room here for these children. We're at capacity now. Over capacity." He tossed the letter on the desk, his lip twisted in contempt. "I will not allow my brother to foist his problems off on me. You can go right back to St. Louis and tell him I said so. How dare he? Without so much as a telegram." He sprang up and shoved his hands into his pockets. "Conrad's a sneaky one."

"Please, sir, we don't have the funds to return. Mr. Korbin—your brother—didn't pay for return tickets. He never thought we'd need them."

"That isn't my problem. These children were perfectly fine where they were, and knowing my brother, it was more than random overcrowding that made him pick these three." He glanced sharply at her. "Ah, I see by your guilty start that I'm on to something. Tell me, what's wrong with them?"

"Nothing, really. They're wonderful children. It isn't their fault. A few physical ailments—"

"Aha!" He pounced before she could continue. "I knew it. What is it? Consumption? The state is overrun with lungers now trying to take the altitude cure. We can't have them mixing with the healthy children in this orphanage. You'll have to take them to one of the asylums."

"No, sir. They're not consumptive. The little one has a bit of a heart ailment, but with medication—"

Again he interrupted her. "Medication? Conrad must think we're made of gold. There's no money for medicaments beyond the occasional dose of castor or cod liver oil. If the child is ill, he should be in a hospital, not an orphanage. What about the other two?"

A hard lump formed in Eldora's throat. "A doctor has written up some case notes. You have them before you there. The little girl, Celeste, is in need of an operation to correct a facial deformity. She's got a harelip, but the doctor seemed to think surgery would put things right."

"Ha!" His bark of laughter made her flinch. "Surgery. Who are you trying to kid? What about the other one, the older boy? What's he got? Pneumonia? Typhoid?"

"No, he's perfectly healthy." The superintendent's derision put some steel into her spine. "There's nothing wrong with Phin that a little love, attention, and kindly discipline wouldn't cure."

"Well, he's not going to get it here. As I said, we're over-crowded and not taking anyone in."

"Please, sir, they've nowhere else to go. Even if you can't afford the medicines or surgery, you can't turn them away."

She gripped her hands until they shook.

"Take them back to St. Louis. If I allow them in here, everyone else will have to get by with less, and we're strapped as it is. This is a private establishment that relies on donations and benevolence to survive, both of which seem to be in short supply at the moment. I'm turning away children every day, and the minute any of the children here turn fourteen, they have to leave to make room for more. There just isn't space. I know you think I'm being cruel, but that's the way it is. It was wrong of my brother to send you here in the first place. How long have you worked for him? You don't look much more than a child yourself."

"I'm nineteen." She lifted her chin. "Perhaps we can reach a compromise. I would be willing to work here for you for just my keep if you would take these children in. I'm well-versed in orphanage life. I can clean, cook some, sew, and do laundry." Impossible to keep the pleading from her voice, but she tried to steady her tone and at least appear professional. "Please, don't turn us out."

His face softened, and for a moment she knew hope, but he shook his head. "I told you it was impossible. You'll think me an ogre, but I've got children sleeping on the floors right now. We're barely getting by for food, and I've got an overabundance of girls here working for their keep as it is. I'm sorry, but there just isn't room. I apologize for my brother getting your hopes up that there would be a place for you here and that he sent you on this hiding to nowhere. Now"—he rose, folded the papers into a tidy bundle, and handed them to her—"if you will excuse me, I've got things to see to."

She found herself ushered out of his office without much ceremony. Five expectant pairs of eyes met hers, and she didn't know what to say. How could she tell these little ones that not even an orphanage wanted them?

"Good night, Miss, er, Carter, was it? And again, I'm sorry I couldn't help you." Mr. Korbin nodded and strode down the hall toward the dining room.

"What does he mean he couldn't help you?"

Eldora clutched the papers in one hand and pinched the headache forming between her eyes. "He says they are full up. There's no room here for us." Her shoulders sagged, and her mind refused to form a single coherent thought.

Phin scowled and shrugged, as if he'd known it all along, and Tick's eyes got round. He slid close and tugged on her hand until she lowered it. He slipped his fingers into hers and gave her a look full of questions. Celeste said nothing, just waited patiently for more of life to happen to her.

"That's ridiculous. I'll be right back." Sam yanked off his hat and marched away, his boots ringing on the hardwood floor.

Buckford's brow furrowed. "I didn't know an orphanage could turn away children in need."

"Apparently they can, especially since this is a private establishment. There's no room and barely enough money to keep food on the table as it is."

Tick squeezed her hand until she looked down at him. "What are we going to do then? Are we getting back on the train?"

She smoothed his fair hair and tried to smile. "We're not getting back on the train. Don't worry. I'll think of something." Though she hadn't a clue what.

Sam came back, his face a thundercloud. "That's it. Grab the bags, Buckford. Phin, give him a hand." He bent and picked up Tick and took Eldora's elbow.

"Where are we going?" She anchored her hat and tried to keep up.

"We're going to my brother's house. I wouldn't leave a dog I didn't like in this place."

eleven

Buckford guided the team to a halt, and Sam looked up at the lighted windows of his brother's townhouse. How would David and Karen react to him showing up with four extras in tow? He braced himself and jumped down. Only one way to find out.

"Come on, kids. We'll have you warmed up in a minute. How does some hot chocolate sound?" He made his voice as jolly as he could, knowing he couldn't make up for their being rejected again. None of the four had said a word during the ride, and he didn't know what hurt worse, the dejection on Tick's and Celeste's faces or the resignation on Phin's and Eldora's.

He shouldered his way through the door, dropping the luggage on the floor by the hall tree. "Karen? David?" Dropping his hat on the newel post at the base of the stairs, he turned to Buckford. "Can you rouse the housekeeper for some hot chocolate?"

Karen appeared at the head of the staircase. "Sam, you're back. I was afraid you might not make it before we left in the morning for Martin City." Carefully, one hand on the rail and the other on the mound of her expectant motherhood, she descended. Before he could make introductions, she held out both hands to Eldora. "You must be Yvette. Welcome to the family." Karen kissed a bewildered Eldora on the cheek. "And who are these young people?"

Sam's innards squirmed. "Karen, I figured Aunt Tabitha would've wired you by now with the news. This is Eldora

Carter, and these children are. . . I guess they're her wards. They need a place to stay tonight. I hope you don't mind. If it's a problem, I can put them up in a hotel." He tilted his head and gave a half grin. Weariness had set up an ache in his muscles, and he lost a moment thinking of how good it would feel to sink into a bed that wasn't rocking and swaying.

A small furrow appeared between Karen's brows. "Of course they're welcome here. We'll find beds for everyone. But where is Yvette?"

"Can we talk about that later? The kids are tired and hungry, and I'm worn clean through. Where's David?"

He and Karen measured glances, and she patted his arm. "We'll talk later. David is in the sitting room. Why don't you take your guests in and make introductions, and I'll see about some supper?"

When she'd disappeared, Eldora put her hand on his arm. "Are you sure about this? I feel terrible, crashing in without warning. Perhaps it would be best if we left."

"Where would you go? Don't worry. Karen and David will welcome you. They're nice people. They'd never turn away three kids in need, especially when they hear what happened at the orphanage."

Sam helped Eldora out of her coat and hung it beside his, then ushered everyone into the warm sitting room. A healthy fire glowed in the fireplace, and the smells of pine boughs and cider wrapped around them. David sat in a chair, his head back on the antimacassar, a heavy book open on his knees.

"Hello, David. I'm back."

His brother sat up, scrabbling for the book before it hit the floor. "Sam? I'm afraid I dozed off. It seems like ages since Buckford went to get you. Welcome back." David set the book on the table beside him, rose, and held out his hand.

Sam grasped it, taking in the content expression and wide smile. A year ago, he wouldn't have given short odds on David's future happiness, but after quite a struggle, it appeared that he and Karen were on a sure footing, at peace and much in love. "Thanks. It's good to be back in Colorado."

"And where is your lovely bride? Karen and I have been so anxious to meet Yvette ever since we got your letter about the engagement. I have to say, you're a fast worker."

Sam squelched a sigh. He should've cabled, but it wasn't something he'd wanted to put in a telegram, and he'd figured Aunt Tabitha would've let folks know. "The wedding didn't come off. But I did bring someone with me."

"How come this book doesn't have any words in it?" Tick turned the heavy cream page. "The paper's all bumpy."

David turned to the voice. "Who might you be?"

"David, these young folks are Tick, Phin, and Celeste. Also with them is Miss Eldora Carter, who is looking after them."

"How do you do?" A hundred questions lingered in David's voice, but he didn't voice them. "And to the one who asked the question, the book has words, but you can't see them. I read with my fingertips, not with my eyes." He smiled. "I'm blind. The little bumps tell me what the words are."

"You can't see anything?" Phin's eyebrows rose. Then he glanced about the room, as if appraising the décor. He shoved his hands in his pockets and looked away when Sam sent him a warning glare.

"I'm afraid not. But I try not to let that slow me down too much." David indicated the chairs before the fireplace. "Miss Carter, won't you sit down?"

Celeste appeared not to notice anything else, having dropped to her knees beside a low table. In the center of the table, a small crèche stood, surrounded by carved Nativity figurines. The little girl had her hands clasped beneath her scarf-wrapped chin, and her eyes were round as pennies.

Eldora perched on the edge of her seat as if she expected someone to yank it out from under her. "I'm so sorry for barging in like this. Sam said you wouldn't mind, but I realize what an imposition it is."

David resumed his seat with a chuckle. "We're used to the unexpected where Sam is concerned. Tell me, how did you two meet?"

Before she could answer, Karen came in with Buckford. The butler smiled at Celeste and winked at Tick. Karen eased down onto the arm of David's chair and took his hand. "Buckford is going to take the children into the kitchen to eat. That way we can visit without interruption."

When the children had followed Buckford out of the room, Sam leaned forward and put his elbows on his knees. "To answer your question, Dave, Eldora and I met at the orphanage in St. Louis. I was there to pick up Aunt Tabitha. Eldora was put in charge of these kids, getting them to Denver, and Tabitha asked me to look out for all of them. You know she's recently joined the board of the children's home in St. Louis? Anyway, due to one thing and another, we got delayed halfway across Kansas for a few days, but we finally made it into town tonight. When we showed up at the Denver orphanage, they wouldn't take the kids. So I brought them here."

Eldora's eyes were bright in the firelight. "I am so sorry, Mrs. Mackenzie. As I told your husband, I realize what an imposition this is. I begged the superintendent to take us in, but he was adamant. They didn't have the room or the money to feed any more children."

Karen nodded her understanding. "Don't worry. Sam did the right thing bringing you here. They just built that new orphanage, and it's already full to bursting. There's talk of adding two new wings come spring. With all the consumptives pouring into the state, and most of them not getting well, the orphanages are filling up quickly." She glanced over at Sam. "Your mother has been approached about starting an orphanage in Martin City. With the central location, it would be ideal for the mining communities. You know how quickly disaster can strike up there."

"That sounds perfect for Mother. You know how she likes organizing people."

Eldora stood. "Mrs. Mackenzie, I should go supervise the children. I don't like leaving them alone. You never know what mischief they might get up to"—she grimaced—"though they are biddable children for the most part. Will you please excuse me? And thank you for taking us into your home tonight. I'll do my best to find a place for us tomorrow." She bobbed her head like a servant.

Sam stood, but his good manners went unnoticed, for she hurried out of the room without a backward glance. He eased down, at a loss to explain her sudden departure.

"Sam, what happened with Yvette?" Karen took Eldora's vacant seat. "We thought you'd be bringing us a bride, and you've brought us three children and a caretaker instead."

A sigh built in his lungs, and he pushed it out. "Yvette turned out to be a beautiful gold digger. She wanted the Mackenzie name and money and didn't care a nickel about me. I was a sucker, fell for her in a big way, and I made a lucky escape, finding out what kind of girl she was before we walked down the aisle." He smiled, trying to make light of it, but it stung like salt in a wound.

David shook his head. "That's too bad. Your letters were—" He stopped, as if not knowing how to say it without making Sam feel worse, and spread his hands, palms up.

"I know. I let myself go on about her, but when I found

out what she was really like, all that outer beauty soured. All I could see was the grasping, money-grubbing dollar signs in her eyes. At that, I don't know who was worse, her or her mother. Hortense Adelman makes a squanderer look like a skinflint. As it is, they weren't just after the money. Yvette came to me at the train station and made one last plea. She's—" His collar tightened, and he grimaced. A bad taste entered his mouth, talking about her this way, but it had to be told. The family deserved to know why the wedding had been called off. If only there was some way to tell it without making him seem such a thickhead. He sighed again. "She's in the family way. The baby isn't mine, I assure you. The father of the child refused to marry her."

The indignant expression on Karen's face gratified him. "You sure made a lucky escape. Imagine if you'd married her." Her scowl softened. "But I have it in me to be sorry for her, too. What will happen to her now?"

"I left her in the care of Aunt Tabitha. If anyone can sort things out, it's her. I imagine she's tracking down the previous suitor, and she'll make him do right by Yvette. Hortense will be appalled, but"—he shrugged—"she's no one to blame but herself, really, raising her daughter to be so acquisitive."

"And how are you taking it? You sound right enough, but it had to hurt." David rubbed his finger along his jaw.

A chuckle escaped Sam's lips. "Truth be told, I've hardly had time to think on it much. Tabitha pitchforked me into looking out for Eldora and the kids, and it seems to have been one crisis after another. There're issues with all of the kids that make them less than ideal for adopting, and all of them came to the fore on the trip."

"What issues?"

"The little boy has heart trouble, which reminds me, we need to get to a drugstore first thing in the morning for more medicine. The little girl—David, she wears a scarf over her mouth all the time because she's got a harelip. It's bad enough that you can't help but be startled by it, but I spoke with a doctor in Kansas who said it was operable. The thing is nobody will adopt kids with problems like that. That's why the director in St. Louis was shipping them out. Seems he was looking for a quick way to get rid of all of them."

"What about the older boy?" Karen rubbed her stomach with her fingertips, a light in her eyes that bespoke maternal feelings.

"Phin. He has a tendency to swipe things that don't belong to him. He's good at it, but not as good as he thinks he is. He gets caught often."

"And Eldora?" A smile played at the corners of Karen's mouth. "She seems nice, and a bit awestruck, if you don't mind my saying so. She never took her eyes off you. Is there something between you two?"

Sam pondered her words. Was it true? Did Eldora watch him? Would he mind if there was something between them? The warmth around his heart mocked him. Though he could easily fall for someone like Eldora, he wasn't minded to play the fool again. And Karen's matchmaking gleam chafed. If he was to court another woman, he wanted to do it himself, not be pushed into it like he'd been shoved around by Yvette and Hortense. Better to disabuse Karen's mind. "There's nothing between us. Yvette cured me of that nonsense by trying to marry me for my money. If I marry someone, it will have to be a girl who is as rich as an empress. Then I'll be sure of her motives. I have no plans to be duped like that again."

A gasp caught his attention, and he looked up from his hands and right into Eldora's big, brown eyes.

❧

It wasn't supposed to hurt this badly. Especially since

she'd warned herself not to fall for him, not to cherish any hopes. She assumed her "institution mask" and stepped into the room, determined that he would never know of her foolishness.

"Have the children finished their meal already?" Karen Mackenzie levered herself out of her chair. At Eldora's nod, she approached and took Eldora's arm. "I'll show you upstairs. I can imagine you're tired out after all your travels and troubles. Sam has been sharing with us some of your adventures."

"It's been a long trip." The tiredness wasn't just of the body but of her spirit, which threatened to collapse altogether under the weight of responsibility and disillusionment. She kept her voice neutral and didn't look in Sam's direction. It mortified her to think that in only a few minutes Sam's sister-in-law had tumbled to Eldora's affection for him. Did Sam know? Was his comment to his family his way of warning Eldora off?

They gathered the children, and Karen showed them upstairs. "You and Celeste can share this room, and the boys can have the room across the hall. Sam will have to bed down on the sofa in the office."

Eldora winced. "I don't want to put him out of a bed. Perhaps Celeste can have the sofa in the office, and I could bed down on the floor?"

"Nonsense. Sam wouldn't hear of it, and neither will I. Believe me, Sam's slept rougher than this." Karen set her lamp on the table beside the door. "The washroom is across the hall next to the boys' room. Why don't we run the kids through there first; then you can have a nice, hot bath."

Phin made short work of his washing up, and Tick followed suit. While Celeste had her turn, Eldora gave Tick his last dose of medicine. Where would she get more for him? If she'd heard correctly, the Mackenzies were all leaving in the morning for the family home in the mountains. Where did that leave her and the children? She'd have to find someplace for them first thing tomorrow.

Tick swallowed down the last drop and swiped his hand across his lips. Even in a few short days, the difference in the little fellow was remarkable. Pink tinged his cheeks, and he didn't stop to rest nearly as often. His eyes sparkled, bright as a bluebird's. He still needed to gain some weight and muscle, but he was making progress. How quickly would that reverse now that they were out of medicine?

"Scamper into bed now, before you catch a chill."

Lying side by side, freshly scrubbed and in warm nightshirts, Phin and Tick snuggled down against real feather pillows for the first time in their lives. "This sure is nice, ain't it?" Tick lifted his chin for Eldora to tuck another blanket in. "What're we going to do in the morning?"

Phin's dark eyes echoed the question, and having had more experience of the trials of life than Tick, those same eyes were clouded with doubts and worry.

Eldora swallowed. "Let me listen to your prayers, and don't worry about tomorrow. The Lord's been taking care of us so far. I don't imagine He'll quit now. Something will turn up." She hoped she sounded surer than she felt. Then guilt pounced on her. Who was she to doubt the Lord's provision?

Tick folded his hands under his chin and closed his eyes. "Dear Lord, thanks for bringing us to such a fine place and for the food we got to eat and for this nice soft bed. Bless Sam and his family for being so nice to us. Watch over us while we sleep, and when we wake up, too. Amen."

Eldora opened her eyes and looked at Phin without raising her chin.

He scowled back and made a big show of dragging his

arms from beneath the covers and lacing his fingers. "What Tick said, I guess. Amen."

She shook her head, her lips pressed together, and then rose and tucked the covers around them once more. "Good night, boys. I'll see you in the morning."

Karen met her in the hall with an armload of fluffy towels and her valise. "I'll just set these in the washroom, and then I want to show you something." Her eyes sparkled. She took Eldora's arm and led her to the bedroom door. Karen put her finger to her lip and peeked around the doorframe.

Eldora peeked too, mystified.

Celeste lay in the high bed, surrounded by a mound of pillows, and in a chair beside her sat David Mackenzie, a book open on his lap, his fingers inching across the pages. "The princess pricked her finger on the spindle, and she dropped into a deep, deep sleep."

Eldora swallowed the lump in her throat. The blind man reading a fairy tale to the little girl was reason enough to choke up, but the tears burning Eldora's eyes were because Celeste's face was bare. The scarf lay folded neatly on the bedside table, and a look of such contentment and joy rested on the child's face as to minimize the shock of her upper lip.

Withdrawing as quietly as she could, Eldora groped for her handkerchief. Karen dabbed at her eyes as well. "Isn't it amazing? Sam said she never takes that scarf off."

"And she never warms up to strangers, but both Buckford and now David have somehow put her at ease. It's uncanny. She didn't unbend for Sam, no matter what he tried, the entire train trip, but here she is completely comfortable with David in only a few minutes."

"It must be because of his blindness. Maybe she feels that because he can't see her face, she's safe to let him get to know her."

Eldora pondered this. "I think you're right. She tries so hard not to be seen, it must be a relief for her to be with David. Maybe she feels he can see the real her instead of being put off by her appearance."

Karen sniffed and dabbed her eyes again. "It's so wonderful to see David like this. One thing he worried about when we first married was what kind of father he would make. Not that he's not thrilled and excited about this baby." She caressed her stomach. "But he's been a little apprehensive. Such a positive response from Celeste will give him confidence." She laughed. "Here I am blathering on, and you must be ready to drop. Have a good soak in the tub and relax a little."

Parting from Karen at the washroom door, Eldora closed herself in the small room and leaned against the door with her eyes closed. Steam rose from the large bathtub, and the smell of roses filled the air. A bottle of bath salts sat on a shelf behind the tub, pink blossoms painted on the label. Bath salts, for an orphan girl?

Bemused, Eldora tied up her hair and slipped into the steaming water of the tub. Immediately, the hot water soothed her tired muscles and leeched some of the tension from her shoulders. A sigh eased from her throat and rippled the water. Never in her whole life had she felt such luxury. Baths at the orphanage were sketchy affairs with tepid water and not much time to wash properly. This was positively decadent—hot scented water up to her chin, room enough to stretch out in the claw-footed tub, a pile of towels waiting.

"Lord, I echo Tick's prayer." She kept her voice to a whisper. "Thank You for keeping watch over us thus far. I admit I don't know what will happen tomorrow, but thank You for a warm place for the children to sleep tonight." A cold stone of heaviness sat just over her heart. "Thank You, too, for opening my eyes to my folly where Sam is concerned. He's made it clear he wants to marry a rich woman and that he would never be interested in someone like me. I knew this with my head, but my heart wanted things to be different. Help me remember to seek Your will and to be content with You. Guard me against the danger of seeking love and approval in the wrong places. Light up the path where I'm supposed to go, and keep me off the paths You know aren't good for me."

Though the prayer was painful, she forced herself to pray it. If only Sam's heart wasn't the wrong place to seek love and approval. She loved everything about him—his smile, his laugh, his protectiveness. The way he treated the children, the way he stood up for them. The memory of his comforting arms around her was something she would treasure always. Realizing she was in danger of turning right back where she had been, she bolted up, sloshing water over the rim of the tub.

Eventually slipping into bed beside the slumbering Celeste, Eldora rolled onto her side and punched up the strangely soft pillows. *Wake up early, girl. You need to find somewhere for you and the kids first thing in the morning.*

twelve

So of course she slept late. Weak winter sunlight streamed through the window when her heavy eyelids opened. For a moment she didn't know where she was, and then the events of the previous day flooded in. A glance at the clock over the fireplace told her it was after eight. She couldn't remember ever staying in bed so long.

Flipping back the covers, she cringed when cold air hit her. Celeste's side of the bed was empty, and her nightgown lay folded on the chair beside the bed, as she had been taught since birth at the orphanage. Eldora hurried, buttoning buttons, pinning up her hair, making the bed. How could she have been so lax? The Mackenzies would be preparing to leave town this morning, and here she was, lazing away. Her stomach rumbled, reminding her of how she'd picked at her food last night.

She poked her head into the boys' room and found it tidy and empty of children. From the first floor, happy voices reached her. Almost tripping in her haste, she made it across the foyer and stopped in the doorway to the sitting room.

Celeste sat on the floor in front of the wooden Nativity figurines. She lifted a donkey and put it in David's hand where he sat in the chair beside her. She followed this action by climbing into his lap and whispering in his ear, lowering the scarf just a bit and then tucking it back up over her nose. David smiled and nodded at whatever she said, and squeezed her before letting her slip back to the floor.

As if this weren't shock enough, Sam and Phin knelt across

from each other on the floor, a string circle between them. Marbles littered the carpet, and Phin shot another into the circle.

Tick jumped out of his chair when he spied her, clutching a book of photographs. "She's awake! Eldora, lookit this!" He hefted the book for her to see. "Pictures of Sam and David and Karen and even Buckford."

"Good morning, Eldora. You look well-rested." Sam sprang to his feet and smiled down at her. "We decided to let you have your sleep out rather than wake you."

Heat tinged her cheeks, and she advanced into the room. "I'm sorry. I meant to rise early. We've imposed on you long enough. Children, please go fetch your things so we can go."

Phin rose slowly and shoved his hands in his pockets, and Celeste's eyes filled with tears, another shock. Celeste never cried. The little girl blinked hard and set the donkey back on the table as if it were made of spun sugar. Both moved to obey her, but Tick held his ground. He clutched the book like a shield and shook his head. "I don't want to go. I want to stay with Sam."

So did she.

Just the sight of Sam, so strong and kind, affected her. She swallowed. "Tick, please. We've imposed long enough. We have to go now."

The little boy dropped the book and belted across the carpet to throw himself against Sam's legs. His sobs rent Eldora's heart, but what could she do? Phin's dark glare accused her, and Celeste edged closer to the door with shuffling feet and bowed head.

Sam bent and lifted Tick into his embrace, and Tick threw his wiry arms around Sam's neck. "Please Sam, can't we stay with you? Just for a little bit longer?"

"Well now, sport, you've stolen a march on me. I was going

to tell you later, but David and Karen and I sat up late last night talking it over. Christmas is only a few days away, and we thought it would be nice if you spent the holiday with us. How's that sound?"

The room reeled, and Eldora clutched the doorframe. Sunbeams shone through Tick's tears, and he hugged Sam so tight his little body shook. Celeste's feet flew, and she threw herself into David's arms with a squeal. David recovered his surprise and patted her back. Even Phin couldn't conceal a grin, toeing the edge of the carpet and ducking his head.

How could she dash their hopes? Each child looked to her for approval, and even more powerful, Sam's gaze pled with her.

He eased Tick down with a pat on the head and approached her. "Let's go out in the hall and talk." He took her elbow and directed her into the foyer.

Wild thoughts, hopes, and guilt skittered around her head until she didn't know which way to hop. Sam had kept her off balance since the moment she'd met him. On the one hand he didn't want someone taking advantage of him, and on the other he repeatedly proved his generosity. It was as if he couldn't help himself. His protective nature *would* come to the fore.

"I know we should've talked to you first, but it seems the perfect solution. You don't have anywhere else to go, and we've got plenty of room at the house in Martin City. My parents would love to have you all. Christmas is always better with children in the house. And think what it would mean to the kids. A real Christmas, not an orphanage one."

"That's very kind of you, but we don't want to impose. We've taken so much of your time and money already. I've no way of paying you back for your generosity. We've been burden enough." Determined, she put force into her words.

"We cannot go to Martin City with you. How do you think we would feel, crashing in on a family holiday celebration? And what would your parents say? You think they would love to have us? You can't know that. Bad enough that your aunt foisted us upon you for the trip."

He frowned and tilted his head. "Nobody foisted you on me. And I do know what my parents would say. My mother would have my hide skinned and stretched on the barn door if I didn't bring you and the kids home with me. David and Karen are so excited about the idea. You'd do us out of this pleasure just for your pride?" Furrows formed on his brow. "Anyway, where else would you go?"

She tugged at her bottom lip. With all her heart she wanted to throw herself into his arms and beg him not to let her go away from him, but she wouldn't. She couldn't. She wouldn't take advantage of him like Yvette had. "I had thought to go back to the orphanage and try to get Finlo Korbin to see reason. If I couldn't persuade him to change his mind, then I thought to try some of the local churches. Then I was going to look for a job."

"A job? Just days before Christmas? Taking care of the kids is job enough. Please, they've got their hearts set on it now." He took her hand and rubbed the back of it with his thumb, sending a quiver through her. Ducking his head, he locked his blue eyes onto hers, entreating her with an engaging, boyish smile. "I do, too."

With a sigh, the resistance fled. "All right, but only over Christmas. Then I have to find some work and a place for the children."

Sam straightened and swung her hand. "Great. We'll sort everything out after Christmas. For now, just relax and enjoy yourself. I have a feeling you haven't had much enjoyment in your life. But you'll see. Problems just melt around my mother."

Corralling the children when Sam broke the good news to them proved nearly impossible. Phin relaxed his guard enough to whistle a Christmas carol while carrying bags. Buckford was dispatched to the closest pharmacy for Tick's medicine, and the housekeeper plied everyone with hot cider and holiday sweets.

Celeste wouldn't be parted from David and insisted on riding with him and Karen to the station in one sleigh while Eldora, Sam, and the boys piled into another. Harness bells crashed and jangled, and Eldora felt as if she were sitting in the midst of a tornado. Buildings flashed by, and in an incredibly short period of time, they were back on the train ensconced once more in the private luxury of the Mackenzie railcar.

The children made themselves at home. Eldora kept watch, wondering what Karen and David would say to their lack of inhibitions. Tick knelt on the sofa and watched out the window, commenting on everyone and everything. Phin dropped into a chair and stretched his feet out, lacing his fingers across his middle and grinning like a cat. Celeste stood beside David's chair.

"Karen, you should get some rest." Sam emerged from helping Buckford stow baggage in the front stateroom. "You've been running around since dawn, and we'll be up late. The train won't pull into Martin City until after ten tonight."

"Karen?" David sat upright, his dark brows bunching. "Are you all right?"

Karen patted David on the shoulder. "I'm quite fine, though a nap sounds lovely. I wonder if I'll be able to sleep though. I don't remember the last time I was so excited for Christmas to come."

Eldora eased Tick's boots off the upholstery, trying

to ignore a pang of guilt. Karen had been on her feet all morning, packing, seeing to last-minute details, all added to because of Eldora and the children. "I'll try to keep the children quiet."

"Don't worry about that. The noise of the train covers most everything else, and even if it doesn't, there's nothing better than happy children's voices." Karen disappeared into the front stateroom.

Turning to the children, Eldora held up a warning finger to her lips. "Regardless of Mrs. Mackenzie's kind words, you will be quiet."

Sam's eyebrow quirked. "Why so chippy? Didn't you sleep well last night?"

She folded her arms. "It won't do for them to forget that they're here on sufferance. They've grown entirely too wild and free on this trip, and though I'd love to see them lose some of their restraint, it doesn't bode well for them in the future. The minute they return to institutional life, they'll be slapped back into place."

His sigh told her he was being patient again. If anything could grate on her nerves like pumice, it was someone being obviously patient and patronizing with her. "You sure are a gloomy Gus this morning." He looked at Phin and Tick. "How's about we let her rest on the sofa, and I'll tell you about Christmas in the Mackenzie house?"

Tick nodded so hard, Eldora thought his head might come off. His slight frame bounced on the seat, barely denting the horsehair upholstery. Phin shrugged, as if he didn't care, but his eyes brightened, and he slid over to make room for Eldora. Celeste perched on the arm of David's chair.

"Now, Dave might have to help me remember some things, but I can tell you, Christmas is quite an event at our house. Our pa is like a big kid. He loves buying presents for people, and for a couple weeks before the holiday he sneaks around wearing a cat-who-got-the-cream grin."

Tick's eyes grew round, and he tucked his hands between his knees and hunched his shoulders.

Eldora bit her lip. Had she done the right thing, allowing the children to have Christmas with the Mackenzies? Not that she'd had a lot of choices. An event like this in their young lives could go one of two ways. Either they would live on the experience and it would help them get through the hard times, or it would start up a hankering in them for the finer things and they would grow bitter at being deprived of them.

She watched Phin, who seemed to feel the injustice of inequality the most and tried to even things up by stealing from those who had more than he did—which was just about everybody. Though he hadn't stolen anything since trying to get medicine for Tick. Or at least he hadn't gotten caught.

"On Christmas Eve, we take the big sleigh with the harnesses all strung with bells, and we drive to the church. There will be candles in every window, and the snow will be deep and make everything seem quiet. If it's a clear night, you'll imagine you can almost reach up and pluck a star out of the sky to keep in your pocket." He made a picking motion over his head. "We'll sing carols and hear about the Reason for Christmas, and we'll all walk outside hushed and reverent."

"When we were kids, we'd hurry to bed as soon as we got home, so the night would go faster and Christmas day would get here sooner." A smile played across David's lips, and for the first time Eldora saw a resemblance between the brothers.

"And I'd lie awake for hours, too excited to sleep," Sam

said. "Then it would be morning, and we'd race downstairs to see what was in our stockings. Whew, the storm's really blowing now." He glanced out the window.

Snow had begun to fall almost the minute the train had pulled out of Denver, and as they rose in elevation, the storm had worsened. Heavy, fat flakes of wet snow had given way to sand-fine particles of ice that scoured the windowpanes and whipped around in the wind.

In the warmth of the railcar, it was easy to push aside the storm and imagine what life must've been like in the Mackenzie household at Christmas. A lump formed in Eldora's throat as she remembered Christmas with her parents in the company-owned house they had shared. . . before her mother had gotten sick and before her father had been killed in the accident at the mine.

"Tell them about the food." David leaned back in his chair, his arm around Celeste to steady her.

"Oh, the food." Sam grinned and patted his stomach. "The house smells so good. There's roast goose and all the trimmings, and pies and cake and candy. Eggnog and hot cocoa. Christmas breakfast is the lightest, fluffiest pancakes you ever saw, drowning in maple syrup and melted butter. And hickory-roasted bacon and ham all the way from Virginia. And just wait until you taste Mother's gingerbread, slathered in whipped cream, warm and spicy. You kids are going to have a wonderful time." He breathed deeply, closing his eyes.

Eldora almost laughed to see all three children and even David doing the same. She had to admit, her mouth watered at the thought of all that wonderful food.

Phin recovered first. "After breakfast what will we do?"

"Well, we'll dig out some of the games David and I used to play when we were kids, and after our dinner has settled,

I imagine we'll go tobogganing. When we get back, all cold and wet and tired, Mother will greet us with hot chocolate, and then we'll start receiving guests. Lots of visiting on Christmas evening. After supper, which is leftover bits from dinner, we'll gather around the piano in the parlor and sing Christmas carols. And best of all, Father will read us the Christmas story."

A father reading the Christmas story. Sam's eyes collided with hers, and she bolted for the passageway before she embarrassed herself fully.

&

For two hours, Sam debated about whether to follow Eldora or give her privacy. He sent Phin back to check on her, but when the boy returned, he said Eldora had fallen asleep on one of the settees in the dining salon. She must be as all in as Karen, who slumbered away in the front sleeping compartment.

The snow continued to blow, and the wheels slipped on the icy rails. Sam whispered into David's ear that the storm seemed to be picking up strength. "Hope they topped up the sand domes. They'll need to sand the tracks, the way it's coming down out there."

David nodded, his face grim. "Surely they'll have the snowplows out on the line as well. The real danger is an avalanche, but they wouldn't have sent us out from Denver if the line were blocked."

Sam scowled out the window while Phin and Tick set up for another game of checkers. "Unless a snow slip happened after we pulled out. I can feel the train plowing through drifts on the track already. If this snow keeps up, we'll be late getting in."

Buckford and a porter entered, each carrying a lunch tray. Fat flakes dotted their shoulders, and icy wind blew in with them.

Sam tossed his paper aside and rose. "I'll get the girls."

"If Karen's still sleeping, don't wake her. She can eat later. I'd rather she got some rest before we get home. You know how it is over the holidays, one event after another." David set down the domino he held and smiled at Celeste. "We'll finish our game after lunch."

Sam found Eldora at the rear of the car, staring out the glass pane in the back door at the caboose. Not much of a view, mostly clouds of snow. She had one arm crossed at her waist, with the other elbow perched on it, her hand across her mouth.

He stopped in the doorway. "Lunch is here. Late, I know, but this way we won't be starving for dinner before we reach home."

She nodded but didn't move.

"Is something wrong?"

"No." The word sounded squeezed tight, like she was barely holding on to control. Just like a female. Something was obviously wrong, and he was supposed to figure it out on his own.

"The kids are pretty excited. Celeste and David are playing dominoes, and Phin and Tick are wrangling over checkers." He shoved his hands into his pockets and braced his shoulder against the passageway wall. Cold air flowed off the bank of windows on his right. Gusts rocked the train, and he ducked to look out under one of the window blinds. "Looks like our white Christmas is guaranteed, not that there was any doubt."

"White and cold."

"But warm and cozy in the house. Mother will love having the kids for Christmas, and Father will be over the moon. David wired ahead and let them know you would be coming with us." He stepped into the room. "You didn't say what upset you back there. Are you still mad about having to come with us?"

She shook her head. "I'm not mad. I just hope I'm doing the right thing. You've filled the children's heads with such grand ideas. Even a simple celebration would've been more than they could've imagined, but the holiday you describe. . ." She turned from the door and hugged her middle. "Reality is going to come crashing in pretty hard in the New Year."

"Maybe, but does that mean they should never have any fun, never have any good times, just because the future might not be so rosy? And who's to say the future might not be brighter than you think?"

"Rosy futures don't happen to orphans very often, especially not these three. This train trip marks the end of your destination. You're coming home, but we're just marking time. You've convinced me to accept your hospitality for the holiday, but after Christmas I still have to find somewhere for these children and myself. The best I can figure is maybe I can get a job as a laundress somewhere—I have plenty of experience as a laundress—and maybe I can find a cheap place to rent—"

The lines on her forehead and the way she twisted her fingers together tore at him, reminding him again of how blessed he had been. "Don't worry about that now. I told you, things will work out." He took her hands and drew her to the cushioned bench along the wall. "What else is bothering you? Maybe talking about it would help."

She lifted her chin in an all-too-familiar gesture that told him he was about to be rebuffed. Again. Then, to his surprise, her eyes glistened, and she ducked her head. Candlelight raced along the coil of her hair, and he wanted to gather her into his arms, to promise her that nothing and no one would ever hurt her. The strength of his protective feelings caught him so off guard he almost missed what she had to say.

"It was when you said your father would be reading the

Christmas story." She whispered, barely audible above the clack of the train and the howl of the wind. "My father used to do that on Christmas Day. It's one of my most vivid memories of him."

She turned those big, brown eyes on him, and his heart raced until he thought he might need a dose of Tick's medicine. "How old were you when you lost him?"

"Ten. I was devastated. I'd already lost my mother to sickness the previous year." She shook her head and tucked a loose hair behind her ear. "We lived in Pennsylvania."

"Pennsylvania? How'd you wind up in St. Louis?" He rubbed his thumbs across the backs of her chilly hands, grateful that she hadn't withdrawn from him.

"Overcrowded orphanages are a fact of life. When there was no more room in the Pittsburgh orphanage, they put us on a westbound train. At every stop, they'd get us off, line us up, and people would look us over for who they would want to adopt." Her delicate throat lurched, and she shrugged. "Nobody wanted me. At ten I was too big to be someone's baby, but I was too small to be of much use around the house. Like Tick, I was skinny and small for my age, and. . .ugly."

"Ugly?" He jerked. "Who told you that?"

"The matron at the first orphanage I was sent to. She said I was all eyes and knees and sallow skin, and who would want a child so morose and difficult anyway? Hair that can't decide whether to be yellow or brown, and dirt-brown eyes don't exactly shout 'beautiful' to anyone." She freed one of her hands from his, touched her hair, and shrugged, but the hurt of those words lingered in her eyes. "When we got to St. Louis, I was the only one who hadn't been adopted, so I was dumped in the orphanage there. The matron didn't think I'd amount to much either, and she was right." Red tinged her cheeks, and she ducked her head. "I can't seem to hold a job, and I can't seem to find a home for these three kids, not even an orphanage."

Her casual acceptance of the matron's summing up of her looks and worth disturbed him. "I don't know what you looked like at ten, newly bereaved and being toted across country, but I can assure you, you're no ugly duckling." Sam tugged on her hand to get her to look at him. Again her magnificent eyes sent a jolt through him. "You're beautiful."

She shook her head. "That's silly. I saw Yvette Adelman at the train station. *She's* beautiful. Porcelain skin, china-blue eyes, and that magnificent auburn hair. She turns heads everywhere she goes. She turned yours. Karen told me about it this morning while we were packing."

His collar tightened, and when she would've withdrawn her hand, he held on. "That was momentary foolishness. I won't gainsay that Yvette is nice to look at, but that's all. She's calculating, scheming, and has an eye to the main chance. She only wants what she can get out of a man, and she's selfish to the core. I feel sorry for her. I'm sorry she got herself into the family way, but I'm not going to marry her just to salvage her reputation."

Eldora's jaw dropped. "You utter cad!" She reared back, yanking her hand away. "What kind of man—"

"Ellie, stop it!" Sam lunged for her and clamped his hand over her mouth. She writhed in his embrace. "No, stop it. You're going to hear me out." Her movements stilled, but her eyes shot sparks. He eased his hand away from her lips, wary that she might burst into scalding speech before he could explain himself. Her nostrils flared with her indignant breathing and she quivered. Momentarily distracted by her nearness, by her pink lips and flushed face, he had to force himself to concentrate.

"I told you not to call me Ellie."

"So you did, and I apologize, but you are going to listen to me. You've had the wrong idea about Yvette from the start." Though he didn't want to, he let his arms fall away from her. "No man likes to speak ill of a woman, but you have to know the truth. Yvette *is* expecting a child, but it isn't mine. I know I can offer you no proof but my word, but I assure you it is *impossible* that the baby could be mine." He stared into her eyes, willing her to understand his meaning and to believe him.

She drew a deep breath and nodded, but doubt lingered, forcing him to go on and admit the entire humiliation of his error in judgment.

"I didn't even know about the baby until Yvette came to the station. From the very beginning she set out to try to trap me into marrying her because I'm wealthy. Her mother brought her up to marry a rich man, and when Yvette found herself with child by a poor man, they locked onto me as the scapegoat, or should I say scape-sheep. I overheard her and her mother summing me up as a dumb sheep, led to the slaughter." He spread his hands. "I admit I was a gullible fool, taken in by her good looks and flattery, but even before I knew what a schemer she was, the engagement was proving to be more pyrite than gold."

"I'm sorry. That's a terrible thing for you to overhear."

"I'm not sorry. I'm grateful. Better a broken engagement than a broken marriage. I only regret being such a mug and getting hornswoggled by their trap. You and Yvette couldn't be more different. She took everything I gave her and expected more—trinkets, flowers, candy. You, on the other hand, won't take so much as a new pair of shoes without fighting me every step of the way." He tilted his head and smiled ruefully.

Eldora rose and went to stand by the windows. By now the snow was so thick and the light so poor it was impossible to make out anything more than a few feet from the train. "You don't know what it's like, always living on sufferance, forced to take charity, knowing that eventually those who are doing their good works toward you are going to abandon you for something else. We learn not to count on others, to rely on ourselves, because in the end that's all we have."

"What about your faith?"

A smile touched the corner of her lips. "Faith's important. Who do you think brings us through when people fail us as they always do? I've been holding on to my faith with both hands this whole trip. I don't know when I've prayed harder."

"You do realize that God uses people to fulfill His purposes, right? If you're praying for help, that help is most likely going to come through someone God brings into your life."

She squirmed and flung her hand out. "I know. I don't—"

Her words were cut off as the train lurched. A shudder rippled through the car, and a horrible grinding noise came from the undercarriage. Sparks illuminated the air beneath the window.

Eldora grabbed a chair, but it gave way under her hand, sending her tumbling into Sam's arms. He held her tight as the coach lurched and rocked, bracing his feet against the floor and his back against the sofa.

Metal screeched and a sound like gravel in a sluice blanketed them. Glass broke and chairs tumbled, and the lamp went out.

thirteen

Eldora was conscious of cold air flowing over her and the rise and fall of Sam's chest under her ear. She fought to unscramble her brain and her limbs.

"What happened?" Hunks of snow and ice bit her skin, and when she tried to roll off Sam, shards of glass tinkled.

He grabbed her. "Be still. I think the window broke. I don't want you getting cut." Wood clacked as he shoved aside a chair and stood, bringing her with him.

Glass trickled off her hair and shoulders, and her hip throbbed where she'd knocked it against something. "We've stopped. Is the car tilting?"

"I think we derailed. Are you hurt?" A match scritched and flared, bringing his face into golden-yellow sight. "We're lucky that lamp went out instead of exploding." Before the match burned too low, he climbed to the opposite side of the car and took down the kerosene lamp. The globe had come off and broken, but the bowl and wick seemed intact. He touched the match to the cotton wick and jerked his hand away as the match burned out. "Ouch." Holding the lamp high, he surveyed the room.

"We've got to get to the children." As she turned to head toward the front of the car, the sound of movement reached her.

"Karen? Sam? Eldora?" David's voice came down the passageway. "Karen? Are you all right?"

"Dave, we're back here. Stay put until I can get to you." Sam took Eldora's hand and helped her along the leaning hall.

"Check on Karen first. The kids and I are fine, just shaken up a little."

Relief coursed through Eldora as she followed Sam. They reached the door to the stateroom where Karen had been napping, but it was wedged shut.

"Karen? Are you all right?" Sam pounded on the door and then handed Eldora the lamp.

"I think so. What happened?" The wooden panel muffled her voice. "I can't get the door open."

"Get back. I'm going to see if I can force it." Sam braced his back against the window frame and kicked his boot upward, crashing it into the brass hasp. The wood around the hasp cracked and splintered. Once more he kicked, and the door broke free of the latch. Using his shoulder, he shoved the pocket door to the side and reached in for Karen.

Her hair tumbled down her neck, and her eyes shone in the lamplight. "Is David all right? And the children?"

They assembled in the front sitting room, taking stock. Eldora's heart gave a pang at the tender embrace shared by David and Karen as they reassured each other that no harm had been done. What must it be like to be cared for that much?

More glass had broken in the front salon, and snow and cold rushed in. Sam shook out Celeste's hood and cloak and handed them to her. "Everybody put on your coats and hats. David, keep everyone here while I go forward and assess the damage. Where's Buckford?"

Phin shook Tick's coat free of glass and helped the little boy into it. "He said there was one more tray to bring from the dining car."

Sam headed for the door. "I'll find him and see how bad the damage is. If it's just our car and the caboose, we'll probably uncouple them and go on."

Eldora tugged on her mittens, trying not to give in to the fear pounding on her chest. If it wasn't just the private car and caboose, what then? They were high in a mountain pass with the snow piling up and pouring in.

She couldn't just sit here and do nothing. "We should marshal our resources here. There might be other people who were hurt. Phin, find as many lamps as you can that didn't get broken and bring them back here. Wedge this table so it is fairly level. Celeste, gather blankets from the beds and be sure to shake them out well in case any glass got on them. Tick, stack these bags up." She pointed to the jumble of suitcases and valises that had tumbled from the overhead rack.

Karen handed David his muffler and slipped her arms into her coat sleeves. "I'll get the medicine kit from the washroom. Eldora, where are you going?"

"I'm going forward to see how bad things are. When I find Buckford, I'll send him to you."

The thin afternoon light had faded toward dusk, but when she emerged from the private car, she could still see the devastation before her. The private car and caboose had uncoupled and lay several yards back from the rest of the train. Through the snow, she made out the back of the passenger car, but it leaned off-kilter, half hanging over the downhill slope to her left. The baggage car appeared to have burst, and parcels and bags littered the mountainside below the train. Where the engine and tender should have been, a mass of snow, rocks, shattered trees, and debris covered the tracks. Sam waded knee deep in the drifts, battling to get to the passenger car. Dark forms emerged through the tilted door, reassuring her that others had survived beyond themselves.

Eldora blinked, barely able to take in the scene. The wind

buffeted her, and she ducked her head into it. The cold sucked her breath from her lungs and tingled against her cheeks. She stuck her head back into the private car. "There's been an avalanche. The engine is buried, and the passenger car is off the tracks. I'm going to help Sam. Phin, you stay here." She held up her hand when the boy started toward her. "David and Karen will need you here."

Floundering in the snow, she fought her way up the incline toward where Sam now handed passengers down to those waiting to receive them. Gasping, she joined the growing group at the rear of the car. "How many passengers are there?" She tried to wipe the snow from her face but only smeared it with her coated mittens.

"Eldora, what are you doing out here? Go back!" Sam scowled at her and tugged his hat on tighter.

"I want to help. Is anyone seriously hurt?"

"It doesn't seem so, though we won't know until we do a head count and assess things. Now stay back. We've got to get them out of this car in case it decides to slide farther down the slope. Help get folks to our car. It's tilted, but it's more secure than this one."

A woman emerged from the back door, and strong hands lowered her to the tracks. Eldora took her arm. "Are you injured? Can you walk?"

White-faced and round-eyed, the woman could only shake her head. "Take my arm." Eldora steadied the woman.

"I'll help you." Eldora looked up into the dear face of Buckford. He had a gash on his temple and a split lip, but he smiled. "It's nothing serious. What about David and Karen and the children?"

"Rattled, but no injuries, thankfully. The private car is the only one that appears to still be intact and reasonably unharmed. A miracle."

"Has anyone seen the conductor?" Eldora let Buckford take the lead, stamping along the path she and Sam had already tread. The woman they helped seemed as frozen as the landscape. When they reached the private car, Buckford directed Eldora to precede him and then handed the woman up the steps.

"I suggest tacking some blankets over those windows and checking the coal stove. Make people as comfortable as you can. Rip up the sheets for bandages if need be." He turned to go.

"Wait! I'm coming with you."

"No, miss. You'll be of more use here."

She knew he spoke the truth, but everything in her wanted to be with Sam.

By the time the passenger car was cleared, they had seventeen additional passengers crowded into the private car. Every chair, sofa, and bed was occupied. Several cuts, many bruises, and one broken arm comprised the injuries. Still missing were the engineer, the brakeman, the fireman, and the mail clerk from the baggage car, all presumed dead.

Sam and the conductor were the last to enter the Mackenzie car, and one look at his face told Eldora that things were even worse than she'd feared.

&

Sam wanted to slam his fist into the florid man's face, but he refrained, clenching his jaw. "You don't get it, do you?" How many times did he have to spell it out before these people would see reason? "There's been an avalanche—albeit a minor one. We can't clear the track ourselves. It's going to take a snowplow from the other direction and an army of shovelers. Every car in this train has derailed to some extent. We'll need a crane to lift them upright again. This train isn't going anywhere under its own power, but it might go right down this mountainside if the rest of that snow shelf up there lets go." He pointed to the up-mountain side of the car.

"I say we wait right here until they can dig us out." The spokesperson—self-elected—from the passenger car crossed his arms and puffed out his chest. His enormous red side-whiskers jutted from his paunchy cheeks like porcupine quills.

"Do you see that snow out there?" Sam waved toward one of the unbroken windows. "At the rate it's falling, we'll be lucky if we don't get buried alive. And the chance of another avalanche grows by the hour."

Crowded into the car like a bunch of canned oysters, shaken and terrified by the crash and the implications, it hadn't taken long—less than an hour—before people began to crack under the strain. Arguments, tears, and now a standoff. The conductor was useless—dazed and silent—and no other train employee appeared to have survived the initial wreck.

Florid-face wasn't done yet. "We've got shelter and some food here and a fire. There are injuries and women and children. We're miles from the nearest stop. We're past due already. Help is probably already on its way."

Sam looked from face to face. Karen and the children huddled close to the stove. Eldora stood in the passageway door, her hand bracing herself against the tilt of the car. "What do you suggest, Sam?"

"The risk of another avalanche aside, there's the issue of heat. We have one hod of coal left for this little stove. The coal tender for the engine is buried in snow and ice. There's not much food aboard, and with more than twenty people it won't last us more than a meal or two, even if we go sparingly. I think we have to try to make it out on foot."

The large man snorted, and his hands flew out in an

exasperated arc. "On foot? Have you lost your mind? Do you even know exactly where we are?"

"We're in Shadow Peak Pass. As the crow flies, we're less than ten miles from Martin City."

"Ten miles might as well be a hundred. We'll freeze to death or get lost in this blizzard."

Several nods and frowns. Those who stood more than a few feet from the stove blew out puffs of frosty air, and the wind howled, flapping the meager blankets tacked over the shattered windows. The temperature continued to plummet.

"We can't leave in the teeth of the storm, I agree. But with the lack of provisions and the imminent threat of another avalanche, I strongly feel that we must go first thing in the morning. There are more men than women, and we can help the weaker ones and the children. In the meantime, some of us should go to the passenger car and see if we can find anything to burn in the stove through the night."

David caught Sam's arm and tugged him close to whisper. "There've been a couple of thaws in between these heavy snowfalls the past week or so. That snow pack will be unstable with sheets of ice between the layers of snow. I'm half-surprised they didn't close the line, but I was so eager to get home, especially for the sake of the children, that I put it out of my mind."

Sam took in his brother's bunched brows and tight lips. "You couldn't have known this would happen. Just be ready to move out as soon as we can. It won't be easy, but I know you're up to it."

"I'm not worried for myself." His grip tightened on Sam's coat sleeve. "What about Karen and the children? I'd never forgive myself if something happened to Karen or the baby or those kids."

Sam squeezed his brother's shoulder and edged his way to

Eldora's side. Her eyes bespoke her worry and understanding of their peril. In that instant, Sam knew how David felt. If anything happened to the women and children—to Eldora—as a result of his actions, he'd never forgive himself. He took Eldora's hand, wishing neither wore gloves so he could feel the warmth of her palm against his and draw comfort from her touch.

She curled her fingers around his for a moment. "I'm worried about Tick. Look how pale he is."

Sam craned to see the little boy. His eyes stood out in his pinched face. "You think his heart is playing up again?"

"The doctor warned us about stressful situations. I don't know what to do. Should I give him more medicine? Less?"

Would moving him from the train pose a greater peril than a possible avalanche? Would the boy be up to a trek over the mountain? Heaviness settled into the pit of his stomach. "I'm going over to the passenger car. I'll be back soon. See about sorting out what foodstuffs we have, will you?"

She nodded. "Be careful."

"And gather the kids and Karen. Put on as many layers as you can. It's going to be a cold night." He gripped her hands. "And a colder tomorrow."

fourteen

"I'm asking you to reconsider." Sam tested the ropes on his improvised pack. "You heard the smaller slides during the night. It's only a matter of time before a big one wipes this train right off the tracks and into that ravine." He jerked his thumb toward the windows behind him that faced the chasm.

"You're the one who should reconsider. It's beyond criminal to take children and women—especially a woman so obviously delicate—out in these conditions." Sam's chief antagonist throughout the past night once again reiterated his case.

"Do you think I haven't wrestled with this from every angle? If I didn't think we were sitting in a death trap here, I wouldn't budge so much as a foot until the snowplows came. But we don't know how many snow slides there are between here and the next stop. They might be days getting to us. With the minor slides now blocking us from the rear, we're well and truly boxed in. No food, not much fuel left, and that ledge overhead ready to let loose at any minute? We can't stay here."

"When one of those children or women dies as a result of your foolishness, I'm going to see to it that you're brought up on charges." The red-faced man, Talbot, crossed his arms and scowled.

Sam turned away, lifting the pack. "Take care, and if you do decide to walk out of here, make sure every group has a lantern and some matches. When we reach Martin City,

146

we'll send out a rescue party."

Seven people waited for him, looking to him to lead them to safety. David, Karen, Buckford, Eldora, and the children. Not another single person from the passenger car had decided to join them. He ducked to peer under the window shade. Snow continued to fall, but the wind had died down. Heavy clouds obscured the sunlight, which would be in short supply in winter in any case, surrounded by peaks as they were.

"Buckford, I'm putting you in charge of Karen. Help her all you can."

The older man's face set in determined lines, and he nodded, putting his hand under her elbow.

Sam turned to Karen. "You'll be sure to tell us when you get tired?"

"We'll be fine." Her tight smile and anxious eyes pierced him.

"David, I'm going to give you the pack to carry. It's not heavy."

"I can take it, Sam."

"I know." He slid the straps onto David's shoulders. "Tick's medicine is in there. Phin, you help David. Let him put his hand on your shoulder as you go ahead of him."

He patted Phin on the head, and for once, the boy didn't scowl and shrug away. His face bore the same determined lines as Buckford's, a mature look that said, "You can count on me."

"Eldora, you take Celeste's hand." He slipped a small packet to her and whispered, "Here are some matches and some of Tick's medicine. I gave some to Buckford, too, just in case something happens and we lose the pack. Better not to have all our ore in one cart, you know?"

Eldora took the bundle and shoved it deep into her coat pocket.

He winked at her and chucked her under the chin. "Don't worry. It will turn out all right."

She nodded, her eyes wide in her heart-shaped face. The trust in her expression both gave him courage and increased the burden of responsibility already weighing on him.

He took up the coil of rope he'd prepared the night before and stuck his head and arm through it so it laid crossways on his chest.

"Now, young fellow. I'm thinking those snowdrifts will be higher than your head. You'll do better if I take you up on my back." Sam lifted Tick onto the edge of a chair and turned around. "Besides, we can help keep each other warm this way." He grinned over his shoulder as Tick clambered up, wrapped his arms around Sam's neck, and tucked his hands under Sam's muffler. "Poke your leg through the rope. It will help you stick on." The boy weighed next to nothing, even bundled as he was. *Lord, please don't let his heart play up.*

Talbot barred the door with his large frame. "I'm asking you not to go. Or at least to go alone and send back help."

Sam blew out a breath and held on to his temper. "I'm not forcing anyone to go with me. They want to go. They understand the dangers. Now, let us pass."

They stood toe-to-toe for a moment, but Sam held his ground, and Talbot stepped aside. Trying not to let his relief show, Sam opened the door and took the first blast of frigid air into his lungs. He picked up the lantern from beside the door, hooked it to his belt, and headed down the stairs. When he stepped off the bottom tread, he sank into the snow up to his knees. "Tick, you're going to have to hang on tight. I'm going to need my hands free most of the time."

"I can walk if you need me to." His voice came through the folds of scarf Eldora had wound around his face.

"Naw, better for you to ride for now. Just keep hold." Sam

turned and helped first Karen and then David down the stairs. Buckford and Phin followed and took up their charges. "I'll go first, then you, Buckford, with Karen. Phin, you follow next with David behind." Eldora emerged onto the platform with Celeste. "Girls, you come last. If you start to fall behind, holler. We don't want to get separated. I'll try to break the trail for you as best I can. If you feel yourself start to slip, drop down on your backside and ride it out."

He stood for a moment on the edge of the railroad bed and surveyed the best way to get to the valley below. His greatest fear was starting an avalanche that would send them shooting down to be buried in drifts. "We're going to angle down and switch back. Stay in my footsteps as much as you can. We'll have to keep a little room between us, just in case one of us does go down, so we don't take the whole party with us. But don't lag too much. Stay within earshot."

With the lantern clanking against his hip, he picked up the length of wood he'd pried off one of the door jambs of the wrecked passenger car to use as a walking stick. As he took the first few steps, he whispered a prayer. "Lord, help us make it down. Keep the snow on the mountain, and please send help for those who wouldn't come with us before it's too late."

Frosty clouds of breath mingled with swirling snowflakes, muffling sound. His boots sank into the drifts, and he probed for good footing before each step. One question bombarded him. Was he leading them away from danger or straight into it?

♈

The exertion of trying to stay upright and keep hold of Celeste's mittened hand warmed Eldora up to the point where she wanted to take off her coat. Floundering in the deep snow, she tried to watch where she put her feet while at the same time keeping her eyes on David's broad shoulders ahead of her. Occasional rocks jutted through the snow that had to be navigated with care, and several times her feet sank down into a thicket or bramble holding up the snow. The branches grabbed her ankles and held fast, forcing her to stop and untangle herself.

"I wish we were wearing dungarees, Celeste." She panted as she freed her skirt yet again from a hidden shrub. They had been picking their way down the mountain for over an hour. When she paused to look back and up, she could no longer make out the shape of the train through the falling snow.

"How are you making out?" David called back. "Is Celeste all right?"

"She's doing better than I am." Eldora blew out a breath and hurried to catch up. "I seem to find every hole and pocket under the snow to fall into."

"Sam!" David called ahead. "I need a rest."

Eldora suspected David wasn't overly tired yet but that he wanted a rest for the women and children. His face had drawn into severe lines. How he must be suffering, unable to see for himself how his wife was doing. And how much trust he had in Sam, and in Phin, too, to lead him safely down the mountain.

Thirty yards ahead, Sam halted and turned to look back up at them. Buckford and Karen reached him, and Karen sagged to the snow with Buckford's help. Tick slid off Sam's back, and Sam jabbed his walking stick into a drift. Phin picked his way down the slope toward them with David on his heels.

A thrust of what could only be maternal pride shot through Eldora. Phin had shouldered the responsibility of helping David like the man he was becoming. His scowls and slouched shoulders had vanished, replaced by confidence and a tender care that made Eldora's eyes smart. The influence of godly men in his life, even after only a few days, was already changing him, opening his eyes to a different way of behaving. If only it could continue past the holidays. How different his life would be if she could find a family like the Mackenzies to adopt him.

Finally, she and Celeste joined the group. Chests rose and fell from the exertion of staying upright, and snow clumped and clung to every fold and wrinkle of clothing. Sweat trickled from her temple, and her knees wobbled. Though used to hard work every day of her life, she'd never exerted herself like now, tramping through thigh-deep snow on such a steep angle, all the while worried about slipping and being hurled down a mountainside.

"We're about level with the treetops now. Soon we'll be in among the trunks and branches." Sam brushed snow from his shoulders and took his hat off to whack it on his thigh. "Good news and bad. There will be better handholds to help us get down, but if we do slip, there's real danger in plowing into one of the trees. You could break a limb or bash your head. Take extra care." He glanced skyward into the falling snow. "It's taken longer than I thought to get this far. At this rate, we might have to camp out. I want to make it down this side and up that ridge before dark." He pointed across to the next peak. "Martin City is on the other side."

It sounded so easy. Their destination lay on the other side, just out of sight. Buckford reached into an inner pocket and pulled out a bundle wrapped in a napkin. "I brought these. Perhaps now would be a good time to enjoy them." Opening the cloth, he revealed four fat oatmeal cookies, a little squashed for being in his pocket.

Tick's eyes glowed, and he tugged down his muffler. "How beaut!"

"Tick can have my share, and Celeste." Phin shrugged and straightened his shoulders, as if trying to appear bigger and tougher than he was.

Eldora's heart went out to him, wanting to hug him but sensing he would be embarrassed.

Sam shook his head. "That's a fine gesture, Phin, but I think everyone should have a bit. There's enough for half a cookie each, and we'll all need every bit of our strength to get where we're going. You eat your share, and don't feel guilty."

Buckford broke the treats in half and passed them around. Tick devoured his in three bites, while Celeste turned her back and broke hers into bites. She tugged down her scarf, popped in a piece, and covered her mouth again to chew. Phin, his brows arrowing toward one another, waited until Sam took a bite of cookie before starting on his own.

Sam tilted his head to Eldora, and with his body shielding his movements from the children, he gave Buckford back half of his portion. Eldora broke hers in half and secreted part back to the butler and nodded when Karen followed suit with her portion and David's.

Tick licked the last crumbs off his fingers and wilted, his shoulders hunched. Though he'd ridden on Sam's back all the way thus far, his skin resembled the snow banks around him, and his freckles stood out like pepper flakes. His breath came in quick, shallow puffs.

"Tick, are you all right? How are you holding up?" Sam squatted and looked into the little boy's eyes.

Tick straightened a little. "I'm fine. I can walk if you need me to. I gotta be getting heavy."

"I barely feel you. Don't waste any worry on me. Better spend the time wondering what you might get in your Christmas stocking in a couple of days. My father is going to love having kids in the house again. He'll probably bury you in toys and goodies." Sam glanced again at the sky. "We'd best push on. Thanks for the cookies, Buckford. They hit the spot."

Buckford nodded and tucked the napkin into his pocket with a private little smile.

Eldora braced herself and took Celeste's hand.

Sam hoisted Tick once more, tucking his leg through the rope. "If you think you're getting too tired to hang on, we can fix up some way to tie you on so you can sleep."

"I'm not sleepy." Tick's heavy eyes belied his words, but she had to admire his courage. "I can stick on."

They set off once again in their straggling line. Following along was hard enough. She didn't know how Sam could continue breaking the trail all by himself. He seemed to have unending stamina and strength. How much would they all need to draw on that strength before they reached Martin City?

The gloom under the trees made it feel like night would soon be upon them, though it was not quite midday yet. Though they no longer switch-backed down the slope, their time didn't improve much due to the sharper incline and the dangerous trees. Sam led them in a straighter line, easing from tree to tree.

After nearly another hour as far as she could guess, Sam halted at the edge of a drop-off. "It looks like this is the best place to go down, but it's going to be tricky. We'll need the rope." He slid Tick to the snow and removed the coil. He tied one end securely around his waist, looped the rope around a tree, and tossed the loose coils down the cliff. "I'll lower you one at a time. Buckford, go first and find a good place for everyone to wait."

Eldora wasn't sorry for the chance to rest, but the thought of dangling down a cliff like bait on a fishing line made her queasy. She couldn't see how far it was, but it seemed an age before Buckford hollered up that he'd reached the bottom.

Sam reeled in the line, and it was Tick's turn. "Sit into the rope, and hold on with both hands. Use your feet to keep you off the rocks as much as you can."

Tick pressed his lips so tightly together they disappeared into a thin line. Sam leaned back against the pull of the rope and played a little out. Tick inched down, out of view.

Eldora held her breath until Buckford's call that the little boy was safely down.

One by one Sam lowered each member of the party over the cliff. Dots of sweat formed on his brow, and his legs shook from the effort of lowering his brother—nearly the same in height and weight—to the arms waiting below to receive him.

Eldora let go of the tree she clutched and inched down the slope toward him. Bracing her feet against the trunk Sam was using for the rope, she grasped the rough hemp.

Sam's jaw tightened. "Take care."

She anchored her boots against the base of the tree and leaned back against the rope, letting it out slowly. Even through her damp gloves the rope made her hands sting. Her shoulders tugged and ached with the strain, but finally, the rope went slack when David reached the others.

Sam used his thumb to swipe at the sweat on his brow. "Your turn next, Ellie."

For once, she didn't correct the use of her name. Drawing a shuddering breath, she allowed him to help her slip into the rope seat.

"Don't look down. Keep your eyes on the rocks in front of you, and try to keep your feet braced. Sit down into the rope." He winked and reached out to touch her cheek. "I won't let you go, Ellie-girl."

With a flash she realized she wished he meant it forever. That he would never let her go out of his life. Afraid her heart showed in her eyes, she closed them. His hands grabbed her arms and gave her a shake. Her eyes popped open to see him nose-to-nose with her.

"Don't go wobbly on me now. You can do this. Are you ready?"

Grateful he took her behavior as fear rather than trying to hide the wave of love for him that cascaded over her, she nodded. Her trust in him was complete. If they survived this nightmarish trek through the mountains, it would kill her to have to leave him after Christmas.

fifteen

After hours of climbing up the other side of the ravine, Eldora knew Sam wasn't trying to be a brute, that he pushed them on out of necessity, but it was hard not to lash back or just sink into the snow and refuse to go on when he urged them to move faster. Her muscles ached, the cold had seeped so far into her bones she wondered if she would ever be warm again, and her mind had long ago grown numb with the never-ending trudging through the drifts.

She thought they would never reach the shoulder of Shadow Peak that they must traverse to descend the slope into Martin City. Everyone needed to rest, but daylight was fading. At least the snow had finally stopped, though the rising wind whipped what had fallen, swirling it around them before gusting on by.

They were just short of the summit when a low growl feathered across her hearing. She stopped and cocked her head, concentrating. The growl grew to a rumble and then a crashing roar. Everyone froze and turned to look back across the valley they'd taken all day to traverse.

Eldora's heart flipped. The enormous snow-shelf on the top of the opposite peak wavered. She blinked as it appeared to quiver in the fading light of sunset. Then, with an inevitable horror, it rushed downward, gaining momentum and sweeping everything before it. Cracking, grating, roiling, the gray-white mass made matchsticks of trees and playthings of boulders. Though she could not see the spot where the train had halted on the tracks, Eldora was certain the avalanche hadn't missed.

Karen cried out and sank to the snow, and David groped his way to her side, cradling her against his coat and rocking her. Phin let out a low whistle, and his gaze collided with Eldora's. All those passengers, so scared but refusing to move. The avalanche would have swept the private car off the tracks like a cougar swatting a mouse.

Celeste stood by David, her hand on his shoulder. Karen glanced up, her face wet with tears, and opened her arms to draw the little girl close. David wrapped his arms around them both. Buckford struggled past them on the path and lifted Tick from Sam's shoulders.

The cascade continued for what seemed a long time, and it wasn't until the stillness rang in her ears that she realized Sam had come to stand at her side. Without a word he slipped his arm around her waist. She put her head on his shoulder, too tired and too numb to cry.

"Those poor people. They were so scared. Why wouldn't they come with us?"

He hugged her and rested his chin on top of her head. "I suppose, for them, the danger of staying wasn't as scary as the danger of going. Some people are afraid to step out along a path when they aren't sure what waits down the road."

"Should we try to go back? To see if anyone survived?" Even as she asked the question, she realized how impossible that would be.

"We have to press on. There's no going back. We're not safe ourselves yet." Weariness and responsibility wrapped his every word. Three children, two women, one of them pregnant, a blind man, and an old man—it was God's grace they'd gotten this far.

"How much farther do we have to go?"

Gently, he turned with his arm still around her. "Look

there. Do you see the lights?" He pointed down the slope toward Martin City. "Those lights will lead us home. That's Martin City. The worst of the journey is over. Just keep your eyes on those lights."

"I've never been so tired in all my life. I can't imagine how the others are feeling." Though reluctant, she stepped out of his embrace and went to Tick, who sat on Buckford's lap with his eyes closed. "Tick, it's time for some medicine. How're you making out?" She tugged down his scarf. His skin had a bluish pallor that struck alarm.

Sam lit the lantern while Eldora dug in the pack for a spoon and Tick's medicine. Melting snow in the spoon over the heat from the lantern, she sprinkled in the powder from a twist of paper. "Take this, Tick. You'll feel better soon." She prayed she was telling the truth. The cold seemed to sap all his strength and energy. His movements were slow and clumsy, and she wound up holding his head steady.

Buckford gave the remaining cookie pieces to the children, winking to forestall Phin's comment. He insisted that Karen take the leftover piece.

"We've got to get moving. As tired as we are, we're liable to fall asleep here, and that would be deadly. The sooner we get down this slope, the sooner we can get warm and dry." Sam kept his voice low. "I'm worried that if we wait much longer we won't be able to go on at all."

They formed a ragged line again. Here on the less-severe slope, the snow was deeper, drifting into piles and heaps. Sam forged ahead, making a path for them to follow. The light from his lantern made dots on the blue-white snow. The clouds parted to reveal an indigo sky sprinkled with stars, and over their shoulders a winter moon rose and bathed the mountainside in soft, white light.

More encouraging, the lights of Martin City lay below.

Warmth, comfort, food. A respite from worry.

❧

A toboggan would be nice about now. The final trek to the Mackenzie house down the gentle incline of what the locals called Sluice Box Hill brought back fond memories of sledding parties that Sam had attended as a youth. How nice it would be to sit down on a toboggan and let it slide them all the way to the base of the hill, as he'd done a hundred times before.

Sam's lungs burned, and he forced his legs to move forward. Several times they stopped to rest, but after only a few minutes, he goaded them on, feeling like an ogre but knowing they couldn't quit until he had them all safe.

He could make out the outline of his parents' home, his memory filling in the details that were too dark to see. Gingerbread trim, turrets, balconies, the widow's walk on the mansard roof. Lights blazed from the lower-floor windows, drawing him forward.

"We're almost there, David. I can see the house." Karen's voice, encouraging her husband even though she must be ready to drop, drifted through the night air. Sam's already-considerable admiration for his sister-in-law grew. Not once on this horrific journey had she complained.

But that could be said of all of them. If kids came any tougher than Phin, Celeste, and Tick, he'd never met them. They soldiered on doggedly, manfully in Phin's case, helping David over tricky bits, taking orders without argument or sulks. Life was like that sometimes, offering watershed moments or experiences that set people on the paths they were going to follow all their lives. Sam knew that with the right influences, Phin would be a son to be proud of.

He nearly tripped at that thought. *A son to be proud of.*

And what of Tick? So sick and yet always optimistic,

always sunny. Lying in a hospital bed or enjoying his first piece of candy in months, the same smile. Bravely clinging to Sam's back as they wallowed in snow or skidded down a slope. Taking his medicine without complaint, and never once questioning why God allowed his health to be so fragile. A family was missing out on a gem by not adopting Tick.

Sam cast a glance back to check everyone's progress. Buckford fought his way along Sam's trail, easing the way for Karen to follow. Behind him, Phin picked his route, searching in the moonlight for the gentlest path. David's hand no longer lay on Phin's shoulder. Instead, Celeste—abandoning Eldora somewhere along the way—walked beside him, helping him and probably drawing comfort at the same time.

The bond between David and Celeste was beautiful to see, the blind man and the scarred girl. Might that not be an answer? If David and Karen had truly lost their hearts to the little girl, Sam couldn't see them letting her go to an orphanage. In spite of the aching cold and exhaustion mauling him, Sam smiled. He might've gained a niece on this trip.

Behind them all, Eldora trudged along, her head down. Even from here he imagined he could see the stubborn tilt of her jaw, the light of independence glowing in her brown eyes. How he longed to batter down those defenses, to make her see herself as he saw her—not as a charity case or an ugly duckling, but as a brave, selfless, beautiful woman.

"We're almost there." Less than a quarter mile to the house. Tired as he was, renewed energy surged through his muscles when he mounted the last ridge of snow and dropped onto the packed ruts of the plowed road. He lifted the lantern higher to light the way.

Finally, Sam led them through the gate and up to the front door. He was so cold not even the rush of warm air that gusted against his cheeks when he opened the door penetrated. The lamplight made his eyes sting, and he blinked. "Mother? Father? We're home."

"Sam?" Mother's voice from the parlor. Something thumped, her skirts rustled, and her footsteps pattered.

His shoulders relaxed, and he eased Tick down onto the chair in the foyer. He braced himself for Mother's embrace, though he was so stiff with cold he could barely raise his arms.

Mother hugged him. "How—where—we thought—"Tears cascaded down her cheeks. "You're alive?"

He stepped to the side, taking her with him. "Not just me. . . look." One-by-one, the rest of the group dragged in, snow-encrusted and cold-numbed.

"Karen, David. . .Buckford!" She blinked, sending fresh tears over the edge, and she clung to Sam as if her knees were giving way. Trembling, her gaze swung back to his face. "Praise God. Your father is in town trying to gather men to form a rescue party."

"We're here. Cold, tired, and hungry, but we made it. There was an avalanche, took out the train. But we can talk about that later. First, there are some folks you need to meet. These are the kids David telegraphed you about, and this is Eldora, who is taking care of them."

"Of course." Mother shook her head and pushed out of his arms. "Where are my manners? Come in, all of you." She called for Mrs. Morgan from the back of the house. "Start running the bathwater and preparing a meal. Then I want you to send one of the maids into town and rouse the doctor. He can check everyone over, especially Karen and these children." Mother burst into action.

On her way up the stairs ahead of Mother, Eldora looked back at him over her shoulder, her eyes filled with thanks but loaded with questions, too. Right now he was too tired to formulate any answers. It was enough that they were safe and soon to be warm.

sixteen

"Eldora, wake up! Wake up! It's Christmas!" A small hand pressed against her cheek and then shook her shoulder.

She cracked one eye.

Tick.

She stretched, her muscles still aching from their snowy ordeal. Pressing her elbows into the mattress, she levered herself up.

"Come on! We're waiting!" Tick tugged on her sleeve, jostling her when she went to rub her eyes.

Phin and Celeste waited at the half-open door, each bundled into a wrapper and slippers. "I've had my medicine and everything. Sam sent us up to get you."

Sam. Her heart beat thick and fast. The man who had saved all their lives had been conspicuous by his absence. When he did return to the house, most of his time was spent with bent heads and private conversations with his brother and parents.

"How is Karen this morning?" She sat up, holding the bedclothes to her chin, luxuriating in the feather-tick and down comforter a moment longer.

"She's downstairs, too. Wait till you see the tree. There's a whole tree right in the house." Tick's eyes glowed like candle flames, and a flush decorated his cheeks. Jesse Mackenzie's surprise was paying off in delight already.

"All right." She grinned and mussed his hair. "I'm coming. Scram so I can get dressed."

With chilly fingers she shoved buttons through buttonholes

and put up her hair. The past couple of days had been a time of drifting, of recovery, and this morning belonged to the children, but by this afternoon she would need to make some sort of plan for their future. She drew a breath against the anvil of anxiety sitting on her chest and opened the door.

Tick grabbed her hand and tugged her down the hall. Phin and Celeste hurried ahead. All four stopped in the parlor doorway. A fir tree, taller than she was, sat in the corner, festooned with paper chains and candles and ropes of popcorn and red berries. Its piney scent reached her, mingled with the spicy aroma of apples and cinnamon.

"Good morning." Sam's mother rose and came toward her. "I wish we could've let you sleep longer, but the children are near to bursting as it is, not to mention Jesse. I'm not sure who is most excited."

Their generosity overwhelmed her.

Sam leaned against the corner of the mantel, a cup of cider in his hand. His cheeks creased in a smile. "Happy Christmas, Eldora."

"And to you." Seeing him, knowing their time together was growing small, was bittersweet, but she vowed not to let it show, to enjoy the morning and face the future when she had to. If their trek down the mountain had taught her anything, it was that God would light her path when the time came. There was no need to borrow trouble.

Karen, bundled from neck to toes in a thick robe and slippers, sat beside David on the settee.

Eldora took the chair next to her. "How are you this morning?"

"Fine. Still tired, but the contractions have stopped. I was worried there for a while, but the doctor says it was the overexertion. If I take it easy, things should be fine. David and his mother have fussed over and cosseted me so much, I haven't lifted a finger since we got here."

David took her hand and raised it to his lips. He leaned close and murmured something against her hair that made her eyes sparkle.

"Now that everyone is here, we can begin." Jesse's voice boomed with good cheer. "We're so thankful that all of you are with us today, we decided to do things a bit out of order for us and start the festivities with the reading of the Christmas story instead of waiting until this evening." The children clustered at his feet as he opened his Bible.

Nostalgia and longing swept over Eldora, taking her back to when she had been a child at her father's knee, hearing him recount the Nativity on a snowy Christmas morning. Back before the orphanage, before the responsibility of these three children, before Sam. Back when she was part of a family.

When she was loved.

When she was Ellie.

At the conclusion of the reading, Jesse prayed a blessing on each one in his household. Then, like a boy, he clapped his hands, rubbing them together. "Who's ready for some presents?"

The gifts rained down. Toys, clothing, books, candy. Her debt to this family increased with each happy squeal. And yet, how could she deprive the kids of this joy when their future was so uncertain? They might as well store up a few happy memories against the time when they must leave here.

It puzzled her that the adults didn't exchange gifts, while at the same time it was a relief, as she had nothing to contribute. Her life in miniature, always receiving, never able to give. Perhaps they withheld their gifts to one another out of deference to her inability to reciprocate. Another kindness from this remarkable family that made her throat thicken.

Each time Jesse handed a gift to Celeste, she took it

right to David and Karen, opening it on David's lap and whispering her thank-yous into their ears. Tick bounced between Phin and Sam, too excited to sit still, while Phin kept shaking his head as if he couldn't quite believe what he was seeing. Every so often he would look Eldora's way, as if asking her how to deal with such bounty. She could read in his eyes the same doubts she felt, as if all this was a temporary dream and reality would come crashing in at any moment. If only she could shore up his confidence.

Sam stayed by the fireplace until the last present was opened and exclaimed over. Shoving himself away from the mantel, he came to stand before the tree while Matilda handed out cups of cider. Sam raised his glass. "Happy Christmas to you all."

Everyone responded in kind and raised their cups.

Eldora sipped the warm cider, breathing in the heady aroma of spiced apples and savoring it on her tongue.

"Now, David, I believe you and Karen have an announcement."

David rose, holding Karen's hand, and reached out for Celeste's. "That's right. Karen and I, with Eldora's permission of course, would like to adopt Celeste as our daughter." He turned his face toward the little girl. "Celeste, would you like that? Would you like to come live with us and be our girl?"

If he could've seen her face, he wouldn't have needed to ask the question. Her china-blue eyes went round, and her lashes flicked over them a few times. She dropped his hand and threw herself against him, staggering him.

A wide grin spread over his face, and he hugged her tight.

Karen wiped her eyes. "I know we should've asked you first, Eldora, seeing as how you are her guardian, but we wanted it to be a Christmas surprise. You don't have any objection, do you?"

Eldora scrabbled for her handkerchief. "Of course I don't.

This is wonderful. I wondered how I was going to pull her away from you both."

They clasped hands, crying and laughing at the same time.

"You know we'll see to it she has the surgery Sam told us about. We'll do everything we can to see she has a normal, happy life. I'm still amazed at how quickly I fell in love with her, but even more amazed at the bond she and David formed almost immediately."

"I know. She's never opened up like that before. I have no qualms about you adopting her. You'll make a wonderful family." A pang ripped through Eldora's heart, and she glanced at Tick and Phin to see how they were taking the news.

The wistful longing in Tick's eyes made her feel hollow and inadequate. Phin had his hands shoved in his robe pockets, and he toed the carpet with his shoulders hunched.

She set down her cup to go to them, but Sam forestalled her. "Glad to know I'm getting a new niece." He raised his cup to Celeste. "And that you're getting a new grandchild sooner than we thought." A nod to his parents, who beamed. "I have a little announcement of my own to make."

Everyone stilled.

"For a while now, I've felt that something was missing in my life. I thought I had found that something when I met Yvette Adelman, but I soon realized what a mistake I was making. When I broke my engagement, I thought I'd just have to live with that empty feeling. Then Aunt Tabitha stepped in." He grinned and rubbed the back of his neck. "When she asked me—or should I say ordered me—to look after a woman and three children on the train from St. Louis to Denver, I thought, 'How hard can it be?'" Spreading his hands wide, he shrugged. "Fights, fainting, arrests, hospitals, jails, avalanches, and treks up and down snowy mountains later. . ."

Eldora pressed her hands together in her lap. Where was he going with this?

Then he handed his mother his cup and squatted between Phin and Tick, putting his hands on their shoulders. "It was when we were almost to Martin City, after climbing and slogging and nearly killing ourselves out there in the snow, that I realized how blessed I was. Part of that empty place in my heart had been filled. Feeling your arms around my neck, Tick, knowing you were fighting to hold on and that you were counting on me. And seeing you, Phin, helping David and Karen and looking out for Celeste whenever you could. I realized here were two boys a man could be proud to call his sons. So, if you're both willing, I want to adopt you. You'll be brothers, and I'll be your pa."

Both boys yelled and flung themselves at him, toppling him backward and making the tree shake and waver. Good thing Matilda had blown out all the candles, or they would've set the house on fire!

While they rolled on the floor giggling, tickling, expressing their joy, Eldora hurried to get out of the room before sobs overtook her. She nearly collided with Buckford in the foyer.

"Happy Christmas." He smiled broadly and shook his head at the laughter and commotion going on in the parlor.

"Thank you, Buckford." She squeezed the words out. "And to you."

Not knowing where else to go, she fled across the foyer and found herself in a dark-paneled study. The windows beckoned. Drawing aside the heavy drapes, she looked out on the snowy landscape. Fresh snow drifted down, adding to the mounds already shrouding the lawn and trees.

Sam was adopting Phin and Tick. They were safe, secure. She should be joyful. She should be in there laughing and shedding happy tears and wishing them well. Her head dropped. Sam had filled the empty place inside of him. But what about the empty place inside of her heart?

Pull yourself together, girl. Don't begrudge those boys their happiness. Crying isn't going to change anything.

Evidently a stern talking-to wasn't going to change much either. She had thought she was alone in the world before, but now she had nobody. Not even three children who needed her.

The door opened behind her, and she straightened, scrubbing her cheeks.

"Eldora?"

Sam.

"Are you all right? You lit out so quickly. You aren't upset because I didn't ask you first, are you?"

"No." Her voice cracked, and she tried again. "No, of course not. You'll make a wonderful family. I couldn't wish anything better for them."

He crossed the room to stand beside her. His very nearness when she had lost him—when he had never been hers to begin with—burned.

She moved away, pretending to concentrate on the landscape through the glass. "They're going to be very happy here. Your family is amazing. First David and Karen adopting Celeste, now you taking the boys. You've made all their dreams come true."

"They're great kids. I meant what I said. Any man would be proud to call them his sons."

"I'm glad you filled that empty space in your heart."

"Did I say that empty space in my heart was full? I said a *part* of it had been filled."

She shrugged. "It won't be empty forever. I venture that someday soon you'll find that rich woman you're looking for."

"Rich woman?" His brow furrowed. "What rich woman?"

"You told David and Karen that if you did marry it would be to a rich woman so you would know you were being married for yourself and not your money. *That* rich woman."

He scrubbed the top of his head. "You have an amazing memory. Are you always going to hold the foolish things I say against me? The girl I've fallen in love with doesn't have a dollar to her name." His hands came up and cupped her shoulders. "But this girl isn't anything like my former fiancée. *This* girl has fought my generosity every minute since I met her."

His grip on her shoulders tightened, forcing her to look up at him.

"Eldora, you left the celebration in there before I could finish what I wanted to say. The empty place inside me won't be filled until you say you'll marry me and make us a family. You're the center of our world, mine and the boys. But it isn't just the boys who need you."

Bewildered, fearing she was somehow dreaming, she stared hard into his eyes. "You've fallen in love?"

A rueful grin teased his lips. "I didn't mean to, but I did. Head-over-heels, don't-care-who-knows-it, can't-stop-thinking-about-her in love." He gave her a little shake. "I want you to forget what I said about marrying a rich woman. That was plain foolishness said to Karen so she wouldn't realize how I was coming to care for you. I don't want a rich wife." He stopped short. "No, I take that back. I *do* want a rich wife."

Her heart plummeted. She *had* been dreaming. Everything went dark inside her, like a candle snuffed in a high wind. She sagged against his grip, but he wasn't through.

"I want a wife so rich in love that she fills our home with laughter and caring. I want a wife so rich in respect and integrity that I'm a better man just for having her in my life." He warmed to his topic, fanning hope with every passing second. "I want a wife so rich in friendship that our years together will fly by, so rich in generosity"—his dear face split in a grin—"that she fills my home with children. The two boys we start with and however many more God blesses us with."

Her whole future shone from his eyes. Light filled every corner of her mind and heart.

"Yessiree, I want a rich wife. You have all that and more to give. I want you to be Ellie again, and I want the chance to show you how much I love you. When are you going to admit that you love me and that we should be together?"

Waves of happiness broke over her. She laughed. "Maybe when you give me a chance to get a word in edgewise. You haven't changed your tactics a bit. Still bullying me with your generosity." With a boldness she wouldn't have believed only a few minutes ago, she twined her arms around his neck and stood on tiptoe. "I want to be Ellie again, too."

His lips came down on hers, demanding and sweet, giving and taking. She responded with everything in her heart—reborn, renewed, loved, and cherished. When he withdrew, reluctantly, a little at a time, she stared into his beautiful blue eyes and returned his smile. Warm tingles shot through her, and she shook her head, unable to believe how quickly she'd gone from despair to delight.

"Are you two done?" Phin's disgusted voice came from around the door. "Me 'n Tick are hungry."

Sam laughed and hugged her tight. "Let's go, Ellie. Our family is waiting."

A Letter To Our Readers

Dear Reader:

In order that we might better contribute to your reading enjoyment, we would appreciate your taking a few minutes to respond to the following questions. We welcome your comments and read each form and letter we receive. When completed, please return to the following:

Fiction Editor
Heartsong Presents
PO Box 719
Uhrichsville, Ohio 44683

1. Did you enjoy reading *Light to My Path* by Erica Vetsch?
   ❑ Very much! I would like to see more books by this author!
   ❑ Moderately. I would have enjoyed it more if

   _____

   _____

   _____

2. Are you a member of **Heartsong Presents**? ❑ Yes ❑ No
   If no, where did you purchase this book? _____

   _____

3. How would you rate, on a scale from 1 (poor) to 5 (superior),
   the cover design? _____

4. On a scale from 1 (poor) to 10 (superior), please rate the
   following elements.

   ____ Heroine   ____ Plot
   ____ Hero   ____ Inspirational theme
   ____ Setting   ____ Secondary characters

5. These characters were special because? _____

_____

_____

6. How has this book inspired your life? _____

_____

_____

7. What settings would you like to see covered in future
   Heartsong Presents books? _____

_____

_____

8. What are some inspirational themes you would like to see
   treated in future books? _____

_____

_____

9. Would you be interested in reading other **Heartsong
   Presents** titles? ❑ Yes ❑ No

10. Please check your age range:
    ❑ Under 18   ❑ 18-24
    ❑ 25-34   ❑ 35-45
    ❑ 46-55   ❑ Over 55

Name _____

Occupation _____

Address _____

City, State, Zip _____

E-mail _____

A Bride's
PORTRAIT
OF DODGE CITY, KANSAS

Deputy Miles Carr has his hands full trying to keep the peace in Dodge City and find a local shopkeeper's killer. When his inquiries lead him to the door of Addie Reed's photography studio, he finds himself more than a little distracted. Does this beauty hold the clue to the killer's identity?

Historical, paperback, 320 pages, 5.5" x 8.375"

———————————————————————

Please send me ____ copies of *A Bride's Portrait of Dodge City, Kansas*.
I am enclosing $12.99 for each.
(Please add $4.00 to cover postage and handling per order. OH add 7% tax.
If outside the U.S. please call 740-922-7280 for shipping charges.)

Name _____

Address _____

City, State, Zip _____

To place a credit card order, call 1-740-922-7280.
Send to: Heartsong Presents Readers' Service, PO Box 721, Uhrichsville, OH 44683

HEARTSONG

PRESENTS

If you love Christian romance...

$12.⁹⁹

You'll love Heartsong Presents' inspiring and faith-filled romances by today's very best Christian authors...Wanda E. Brunstetter, Mary Connealy, Susan Page Davis, Cathy Marie Hake, and Joyce Livingston, to mention a few!

When you join Heartsong Presents, you'll enjoy four brand-new, mass-market, 176-page books—two contemporary and two historical—that will build you up in your faith when you discover God's role in every relationship you read about!

Imagine...four new romances every four weeks—with men and women like you who long to meet the one God has chosen as the love of their lives...all for the low price of $12.99 postpaid.

Mass Market 176 Pages

To join, simply visit www.heartsong presents.com or complete the coupon below and mail it to the address provided.